I0556346

Also by Becky Varley-Winter

POETRY:

Heroines: On the Blue Peninsula (V. Press, 2019)

LITERARY CRITICISM:

Reading Fragments and Fragmentation in Modernist Literature

(Sussex Academic Press, 2018)

BLOOM

Varley-Winter

ISBN: 978-1-913642-74-7

Cover design by Aaron Kent

Edited & Typeset by Aaron Kent

Broken Sleep Books (2021)

Broken Sleep Books Ltd
Rhydwen,
Talgarreg,
SA44 4HB
Wales

Contents

Bloom

Becky Varley-Winter

White Truck

Song: Ca' the Yowes to the Knowes, cover by Joanna Newsom

I am looking at a dusty white pick–up truck with thick mud on the wheels, the colour of terracotta clay. The mud clusters on the treads in big red clots.

This truck is in the wrong place.

I know every car on this darkening road, and when they come and go. I give them permission to do so. If I looked at my neighbour driving past and said "Stop," his car would make a dull rattling strangled sound, then it would stop.

I only let them come and go because I am so kind.

My hamlet is small and high up, on a single narrow road where the cloud collects over the valley. Some neighbours left long ago, after the mines closed. Their houses are claimed by brambles, and by the red hips of the dog roses.

Now that it is winter, I shelter in my bungalow most of the time. The garden is surrounded by tangled brush that glows like orange fire in the midwinter light. This shades into pine trees, dropping pinecones that creatures gnaw on in hunger or malice, then you see the wide and purple moors. Beneath, the earth is riddled with hidden pits.

The road is bad, which I approve of. The Wi Fi is also bad, I am told. This discourages visitors. "Oh," they exclaim, lost, waving their smooth squat wands in the air like divining rods. "Where's the Wi Fi?"

I do not need the Wi Fi. It is cursed.

If I require supplies, I walk down, into the valley, to the Post Office Shop, moving quickly, keeping upright. I do not stay long.

Opposite my bungalow is the cottage where Peter lives. It is grey stone, with ivy crawling over the step, and the forest crowds darkly behind it. The white truck is now parked outside Peter's house.

It must belong to my enemy.

My enemy works against me and is always changing shape. He can become a cumulus cloud, a spider descending slowly from the ceiling, a gibbous moon, a baby's face. He has taken people I love. When he is invisible, that is when I am afraid. I prefer things to stay where I can see them, and not change.

I am standing before the enemy's truck with anger filling my body. The urge to slash his tyres is granular as sand, flowing into me like the lower chamber of an hourglass, when somebody says, "Hello?"

A man's voice. The enemy, it must be. I keep my eyes on the clogged wheels as his footsteps approach.

"Do you need me to move my pick–up?" he says.

I feel him looking at me.

"That mud's thick, eh?" he says. "There was such a storm when I was driving up last night, I couldn't see. Was afraid I'd get stuck, then I'd be in a right state. Bad reception up here."

I silently count the stones in the mud.

"I've come to see my dad, Peter. You know him? He moved back here a couple of months ago."

I stay silent.

"He's sick, you see. Didn't tell us, wouldn't call the doctor. Stubborn git."

I do not react.

"…Well. I should go back in. Are you okay?" He laughs a small infuriating laugh, and at this I turn, indignant, searching for a retort.

My voice dies out; the enemy is not as I expected. With terrible cunning, he has taken the appearance of Peter's son, who looks much as Peter did in his youth. He wears the mild expression of a sloth. This disguise is meant to touch me at my weakest. Well! He will not trick me. I meet his eyes with silent fury.

"Okay," the enemy says, making a face. He retreats, raising his arms in a surrender gesture, back towards Peter's house.

Peter and I were children together. Once we leaped, shrieking, from Peter's oak tree into the brambles, then crawled out, bloody and smeared in blackberries. His mother called me a bad girl and a bad influence. I remember the small thorns caught in my skin, and the bruises covered in purple stains, like an outward sign of badness inside me.

I return to my bungalow, feeling troubled. I have faced the enemy, yet the white truck is still on the street. Also, Peter is unwell.

It is a long time since I last talked with Peter. I've avoided seeing him. I know that I look changed, though my hair still has black beside the grey, and my eyes are as blue as they were when we were eighteen, when Peter and I walked together into the moors. That day I was tired from crying, as my mother was Not Herself again. We entered a sharp scrub of gorse. The gorse bushes were covered in fevered yellow flowers. We stayed there until dark fell, and the wind rattled dry branches all around us. That night Peter held me with my back curled against his chest, and my breasts cupped in his hands.

I will make Peter a healing broth and deliver it to him even under the eyes of the enemy.

I simmer the broth: Onions, Garlic, Mint, Lemon, Pepper, Salt, Stock, the Flesh of a Chicken. I carry it in the lidded pan slowly carefully through the blue evening to Peter's house.

My enemy opens the door.

"I am here to see Peter," I say.

"Mary," he says. "Dad said he knows you. Come in."

I step warily over the threshold into the porch. The tile behind the doorbell has kept its design, a fountain of purple flowers. This was once the home of Peter's parents. Now it is his. I have not been inside it since I was young, and I am pleased that it has not changed.

I enter the house with dignity.

"What's in the pan?" asks the enemy.

"Broth," I say righteously.

"That's very kind."

"It's for Peter," I say.

The enemy ladles the broth into a blue bowl. I watch to see that he does not poison it, then take it quickly away from him.

"Mary?" Peter calls. I approach with the steaming bowl and place it before him. He smiles at me. "It's been so long. How are you?"

I gesture that the enemy must leave. He meets Peter's eye before retreating. I look at Peter and nod meaningfully. "The enemy is here."

"Is he? I hope I'm not your enemy, Mary."

"No," I say, "but he is very close."

Peter has a half–amused, half–sceptical look which I know well. We have many means of denying the truth. His breathing is laboured.

I lay my hand on his, to show that I will protect him. "Eat," I say. He lifts it to his lips, blows, sips.

"Very nice," he says. "Like your dad used to make, in winter."

"Yes, the same."

"I was sorry when he died. That must have been hard, so soon after your ma had to go to the Priory."

I nod. "It was the enemy's fault."

"This enemy sounds like a fearsome fellow."

"He is," I say.

Peter looks at me sadly. "I'm so sorry I didn't come back up here then, for the funeral. To pay my respects. I didn't think Orla would like it. Me seeing you, you know."

"I did not expect you to come," I say.

My face is hot. A lie. I had expected him.

"It was silly," Peter said. "We broke up anyway. Afterwards it felt too late to say, how sorry I was."

"It's past," I say. "Eat."

He eats as I sit rigidly on the sofa beside him. His ancient cat nuzzles my head.

"I've been looking for you when I was out," Peter says. "I thought you were hiding from me. Were you? I knocked but you wouldn't answer."

I put my hair in front of my face. "I did not look my best."

Peter laughs. "Is that it! Christ, I thought you hated me. Mary, you're my oldest friend. I don't care what you look like."

I let my hair fall back, and he inspects my face. "You always look okay to me. Maybe you could use some sun. I hope you'll stay for a bit?"

"I will stay here tonight," I say. As protection.

"Dad," the enemy says. He's in the doorway. "Is she all right?"

"It's all right, Danny," he says. "She's okay."

The enemy is confusing me. He is not behaving as I expect. He looks humbled, and has brought me tea. Also a biscuit.

Danny.

"Let's see what's on the telly, shall we?" Peter says. He flicks through channels. I hold his other hand and feel the light pulse through his skin. Nothing will take him, not while I keep watch. The cat purrs loudly into the back of my head and the vibration of it spreads outwards, in rings.

The Psychic

Song: *Aquarius / Let the Sunshine In* by The 5th Dimension

Lola had complete faith in her dreams, which told her the truth.

For example, one night she dreamed that her husband was having an affair with her best friend. She walked in on them both just as his tongue was entering her cunt. *Oh, hi Lola,* her friend said, without surprise, and Lola's husband looked up with a mild, answering–the–door expression, his chin still wet. *How could you be so inconsiderate of me, of my feelings* Lola shouted, but in the stifled voice of dreams. When she slammed out of the flat, her front door was perched at the climax of a chalk precipice. She sat with her bare feet, covered in chalk dust, dangling over the edge, and watched the sea break far below.

She woke to her husband snoring soundly. She considered shaking him awake, but her vision was clear.

That morning she acted as though nothing had happened, although her heart was broken. Her husband was hunched over the toaster with his face still full of sleep. She looked at his dishevelled hair, the familiar mole on the back of his neck, the delicate bones of his ankles, and swallowed.

"You're quiet," he said, touching her curls.

"I'm just tired."

"We're all tired these days."

Lola didn't reply. Outside, the 7am June sky was white as a sheet.

She kissed him goodbye at the train station, where they usually went to work in opposite directions, and watched him step aboard his train.

She waited on her platform, but instead of travelling into work as she usually did, she took a train directly towards the sea.

On the way, she texted her boss to explain that she had a personal crisis to attend to and she didn't know when she would be coming back. She said she hoped they would understand, though she knew that they would not. It was hard to fathom destiny. She turned her phone off and gazed out of the window at the graffitied landscape rushing away, into pitching downs and pale streamers of fog.

The seaside town was bright and calm and chipped. Lola walked downhill, past cafés steaming into life, beneath crying, wheeling seagulls, then sat on the pebbled beach and looked out at the ocean, waiting for it to give her a sign.

It was still early morning. The clouds had cleared, letting through some diluted sun which intensified, slowly, to glitter on the horizon.

Lola stood up, stretched, stripped off her work clothes, folded them on the stones, and walked in her underwear into the cold water. She was submerged and shivering. As she waded, her foot struck a sharp outcrop of rock, but the waves numbed her pain. She unhooked her bra and let it trail behind her, then lay on her back and closed her eyes. The water moved like fingers through her hair.

Long ago she had a boyfriend here who she loved helplessly. He didn't love her back, or not enough to tell her so, and not all the time. Around him her thoughts melted into the heat of her needs, she was hungry but had no appetite, and slept badly. It was no sustainable way to live.

One night she dreamed that she walked naked for miles, over cracked concrete and gravel and dust and grit, to reach his front door. He opened it and said quietly, *Oh Lola, you can't stay here*, then he carried her back the way she came, cradled against his chest. In the dream he was like a giant, and so apologetic about his inability to love her in the way she needed to be loved that she couldn't even be angry. She knew it was really over then. That was the beginning of her faith in dreams.

Now, floating on her back, she cried nostalgic salty tears for her lost life.

She had first seen her husband in a club, dancing. The lights gleamed over the sheen of sweat and covered his skin in morning dew. She felt her breathing move into a more comfortable rhythm just by looking at him. He had an amused intelligent face. She watched him at the bar, silhouetted in flashing neon, and thought if that man looks back at me in five seconds' time, I'm going to marry him. Five, four, three, two, one…

He looked back. How could fate send her such a false sign?

She sighed and propelled her way back to shore, moving her arms gently like a sea anemone. It was so early that only a few people were out, and none were close enough to shout at her, mock her, stop her, or any of the other things that people do to naked women. She wrung out her wet bra, clipped it, and pulled on her work clothes, then slopped up the beach to a vintage shop on the sea front. She bought gold leggings, a pink shift dress and silver sneakers, with her hair dripping on to the counter.

The cashier asked suspiciously if Lola was all right and she said yes, of course. With these clothes she would start her new life. She took off her wedding ring and put it inside her purse.

She explored the town all morning, drifting from souvenir shops to cafés, then entered a small shadowy bar with a Staff Wanted sign. Her outfit seemed to impress the barman, who gave her a trial shift straight away. His name was Lucas. He taught her how to make mojitos, from which he took small minty sips throughout his shift. He was so fascinated by alcohol — its ingredients, the colours, the deft twists of sugar and lime on the rim of the glass — that she wondered if he loved it more than he could love any person, but his eyes were as grey as the sea in her dream, which she was sure must be a good sign.

At the end of the night, they dried glasses together, and Lucas asked where she lived. She said, "Nowhere, I just got into town."

He blinked and asked where, exactly, she planned to get a hotel at this time. She said brightly that she would find somewhere.

Well, he said, she could crash on his sofa that night if she wanted to. He lived in a flat above the bar. It was clean.

Upstairs he offered her a nightcap and she said no thanks, so he said well, tea then. She sipped tea on his sofa with his small dumpling-shaped dog, Bessie, curled beside her and a scratchy wool blanket around her shoulders.

After a long expectant silence, Lucas said goodnight, then retreated into the dark hollow of his room. The flat was small enough that Lola could hear him breathing and sense the warmth of his sleep emanating through the door.

This continued for two more nights. When Lola wasn't working with Lucas in the bar, she walked Bessie and swam in the sea, then sat in the cafés reading second–hand paperbacks, turning the leaves with clean salty hands. She kept her phone switched off.

As she read and stopped and glanced out of windows at the sea, memories of Maria kept surfacing. Maria was Lola's best friend, who she had last seen with her husband's head trapped between her thighs. When Lola thought about Maria she had to put her book down, and her coffee went cold.

Maria had a gift for intimacy and a full rich laugh that echoed through rooms and made people turn towards her like the sun. She created, through friends, the love that her childhood hadn't returned to her. Sometimes she had panic attacks. When that happened Lola held her hands to stop them from shaking and brushed her long wavy hair away from her face. Maria was like a sister to her.

Lola had thought that her husband was also protective of

Maria. She remembered him bringing Maria her coat at the end of long evenings at their flat, holding the coat up by its sleeves in the shape of a crucifix, and Maria disappearing into it.

Lola considered hurling her phone, still switched off, into the waves, but didn't feel ready. Instead, she thought about Lucas. He skewed their conversations towards her so instinctively that it was only clear afterwards that he said nothing about himself. He had, she thought, low self–esteem.

"I want to know about you," she said, on the third night, as they were drying glasses together in the closed bar. "Tell me anything. What's your favourite film?"

"Oh I don't know," he said. "Transformers?"

She laughed and he echoed her, uncertainly. "Is that funny?"

"You're in your thirties," she said, and reached to tuck a strand of hair behind his ear.

He put down the glass he was holding, with a jolt. A crack ran through it. "I like action," he said, and kissed her clumsily. Soon she was up on the counter in the shuttered bar and he was pulling her tights apart. Sex was uncomfortable on the hard surface but he kept saying "oh my god, oh my god" as though this was the most amazing thing ever to happen to him and she was so touched by this that she cried into his neck. He asked if he'd done anything wrong and she said no, she was just overwhelmed, at which he looked pleased and proud although she'd meant, emotionally speaking.

He kissed her on the forehead and Lola imagined reassembling the blocks of herself into a new, as–yet unknown shape.

That night she lay awake beside Lucas's breathing, his arm flung over her like a heavy rope. When she finally slept, she had the last and worst dream. Her husband was crying and wailing in the corner of Lucas's darkened room, *Where are you? Are you dead?* and his voice was apocalyptic with sadness. His eyes looked bruised.

She wasn't sure if she was dead or alive. She might now be

a ghost. When she got up and looked into the cracked mirror over the sink, her face was vanishing into a sea mist.

This dream was a very clear sign, erasing all previous signs, so in a sweat she kissed Lucas's sleeping shoulder, left a note saying thank you for all of his troubles, but it's over, and do not look for me ever, signed it *Lola xxx*, put her ring on her finger and walked back to the cold station, to wait for the first train at dawn.

Trinity

Song: *Personal Jesus*, cover by Johnny Cash

While we were out, my mother installed the porcelain Jesus on the mantelpiece over our bed. He looked like he was holding a cup of tea in his clasped hands – to sip in judgement – and his hair was peroxide blond.

We gazed up at Jesus. When the bedside light was on, his shadow spread behind him like the mountainous dong of God.

You were unhooking my bra. "Do you think Jesus is into three–ways?" I asked.

"He seems open–minded," you said, and gently turned Jesus to face the wall.

I had to keep my raptures low.

"We need to get out of this house," I said, "before good–time Jesus kills us in our sleep."

That spring, my mother was certain that the Rapture was coming soon. I had to admit, this time, it made sense. There had been so many signs. Fires and floods, and locusts spiralling into huge tornado–shaped hosts, their wings translucent as dirty windscreens. Finally, the pestilence. Talk of end–times bubbled from our mouths with desperate levity. We laughed like hyenas.

My mother sat, rapt, in front of YouTube, watching the locusts munch through crops with obvious demonic energy, and she prayed. Mammon and Beelzebub were gnawing the heads off vampire bats. What else could explain these motes flailing in the air?

Religion was the only love that she believed was everlasting. She was devoted to salvation, and put reminders of it everywhere, with innocent passion, like a girl surrounding a boy's name with hearts: the Father, the Son and the Holy Ghost.

When she returned from Lidl, we were watching TV innocently in the sitting room, but I knew that she knew we'd been doing pagan things in the house. She shook her head in silence and sat down beside us.

We were watching a terrible dating show about strangers locked together in isolated cubicles, sweating and losing their minds, until one of them, in a blind panic, gives in, and proposes marriage.

"When are you two getting married?" she said. She tapped my thigh.

"We don't believe in it," I said.

"You don't believe in anything. One day you'll be on your knees in front of God, completely helpless."

"He'd love that. Mary didn't consent," I said.

She half–laughed in shock, then slapped me. I felt you flinch beside me, though it wasn't a hard slap. Almost affectionate.

"Ow," I said.

"Have some respect," she muttered.

"If you believe in marriage, what happened to you and dad?"

"God, give me strength," she said, turning the TV up.

When I came downstairs the next morning, she was absorbing a YouTube show on the many elaborate hoaxes of medicine.

Cure yourself with lemon juice and sunlight, the presenter's smooth voice assured us. Needles were never meant to go into anybody's arms. What were we, voodoo dolls? Puppets of the state?

The presenter was extremely pale, as though all her blood had turned the colour of lighter fuel. She looked worn out by transcendence. "Trust your body," she said. "It knows what to do."

Mum nodded, comforted.

Of course she didn't wear a mask over her nose and mouth. It wasn't natural.

"*Death* is natural," I said.

"When it's my time, it's my time," she said.

"No," I replied.

I scorned her, yet I understood. There is a perverse sense of freedom in capitulation. Fuck me up, kill me if you can. Amen.

My body always knew what to do with you.

"Would you really hate to get married?" you asked, sometime after midnight. The moon streamed through the window over the gleaming robes of Jesus. Our bodies were outlined in white light, like pearls.

I smiled. In shadow, I couldn't make out your face, but your voice sounded soft. You were one of few promises I was sure of.

"After the pestilence?" I said. "Yeah, ok."

We kissed and laughed in the same breath, as though giving each other life support.

"Don't tell her," I said. "She'd never let me forget it. We'll elope or something."

I hoped, but didn't believe, that the pestilence would really end. This was the only life I could foresee, unemployed, skint, trapped in the gap between what we could be, and what we were.

Outside, great conflagrations, circular movements of people scattering across the earth, and no room at any inn. Under such circumstances, even I cried into the damp pillow of Faith. I looked up at the trippy, ridiculous face of porcelain Jesus, his features now blotted out by night, and thought, oh God. Save us if you can.

Taste

Song: *All Along the Watchtower*, cover by Jimi Hendrix

When she bit into the dove it tasted like burnt metal and tyres screeching on late deserted roads.

This was a new country now, and they were all living with the dead birds. Their bodies lay on every street, spread out like x–rays of constricted chests, of lungs, with spectral breath emptied from their bodies.

Not wanting to waste it, she gathered up the dove, roasted it, and picked its bones clean.

The Sky Gate

Song: *Moments of Pleasure* by Kate Bush

Afterwards she picked up her life like threads to be woven later.

She was very able to boil a kettle. Funerals reminded her of plays with their lights and plinths, and she did not cry.

Tea stewed fragrantly in the cup. She combed her hair in front of the mirror and watched the strands separate, crackling. She washed her sheets, smelled them and lay down, carefully clean, like an apple wrapped in white paper.

She didn't wash the pillows; she could still smell him there. She fell asleep on her side with her hands clutching the sheet.

By morning she was wound up in the sheet, her eyes were glassy and dry, and she could not remember her dreams.

The house was so quiet that she went out for a walk. Her limbs felt stiff, her mouth gummy as the back of a stamp. The house seemed to watch her go.

She started to think that maybe she should go away. She thought of blue lakes through a window, and sun–struck streets.

At the top of the hill she looked up and saw an enormous flock of starlings. They contracted like the fingers of one hand, a large hand closing over her in arranged panic, a cyclone of noise, an avalanche, ash.

She opened her mouth to exclaim, and her face froze into a fish–gape. She must have looked so funny. She felt her face crack like two shelves of rock that slide apart, two clouds racing away from each other, the gape of sky towards which breath fled, a dry heave of space.

Her nose was pressed in the grass. It smelled like sheets or sheets smelled like grass. Her body clenched and unclenched like a clam or a crab on its back. Shadows of clouds raced over her, shadows of birds getting further and further away, through the sky gate.

Never Would I Ever

Song: *The Real Thing* by Russell Morris

He dared her to touch the electrified fence that ran along the edge of the farm. She looked at him as she held it, feeling its nerve tense. It didn't jolt but trembled in her clenched fist. It was like standing naked in front of him.

They walked together along the top of a steep ravine that meandered down to the beach. It brimmed with woven branches, dark green leaves and creepers tangled together like bawdy tattoos.

She remembered wanting him so much that it felt like panic. I want you so much, they had said to each other in the dark.

Now she had tamed her body until it was her own domain. She could decide which feeling to listen to, what to say.

They looked down into the ravine, obscured by wild debris. Somewhere at the base of it was an invisible stream.

"If I pushed you in," he said contemplatively, "You'd never get out. You'd be stuck."

He liked to joke about suffering – falling downstairs, deadly plagues, drowning – and she'd laugh, shocked, fighting the urge to cross herself or throw salt. She was afraid that saying bad things too loudly could bring the spoken thing to life. He spoke casually, as though to inoculate himself against that possibility.

She thought, although she could not prove it, that men were better at separating words from what they described. She reminded herself that real feelings were not contingent on what you said about them, or on any kind of expression. They rose up, then vanished again, like monster fish breaking the surface of the sea.

Still, the image of herself trapped in the gnarled branches below, speared by them, frightened her.

"Would you really push me into a ravine?" she asked. They had stopped walking and were sitting on a skeletal wooden bench, facing the land's end.

"Are you actually worried about that?" He was watching the horizon.

"Yes," she said, shivering. "Or, not even that you would. That you'd like to."

A grey wind whipped over them.

"Could anyone ever want to hurt you?" he said. "I can't imagine it."

Then he flicked her lightly with the twig he was holding, swatting her like a fly.

"Ow!" she said, feeling it. It buzzed against her skin. She sat completely still, letting the sensation trail through her, an unearthed wire.

Stones

Song: *Silence* by PJ Harvey

"This is going to hurt," the nurse says.

"I know," I reply.

The stones are huge and mottled, dense as anvils, but round and even. There is nothing grotesque about them, although they frighten me. Their smooth surfaces have an austere and undeniable beauty.

Do not misunderstand me, I have no morbid attraction to pain. However, I understand that it's part of nature. These stones look carved by the sea.

"Are you ready?" the nurse asks.

"If I'm ready," I say, "will it hurt less?"

"No, but it will go more smoothly. It will be a smoother process."

"I'm ready," I say, and prepare to receive the stones.

As soon as the first stone is placed on me, I know I was not as ready as I believed. The nurse holds me down and I start to cry.

The first stone she places on my pelvis, the second on my chest, and the third, a smaller stone, in the centre of my forehead.

I am sinking into the earth.

"Stay,' she says. "Breathe."

I breathe. It's difficult. Stones are on me. The nurse places one hand, cool and dry, on my cheek. Her eyes are kind.

The Pregnant Statue

Song: *The Barrel* by Aldous Harding

In the grounds of the castle there was a pregnant statue. Kora looked at it, lightly touching her own stomach. The statue smiled down at her, replete with stony life. Hydrangeas surrounded it, glossy with dew, and ivy trailed over its belly, suckling with pale mouths.

The statue had lived for centuries in that suspended state, waiting for its stone belly to crack, and for the ivy to crawl in.

Kora had always believed that she would have a baby. That was just how the story went. Now she only believed in chance.

They'd never tried, but there were scares. Once she was a full week late. In those uncertain days she felt like a direct window on to the universe — its haywire galaxies — as spring rose around her, heightened and ecstatic — then the blood came, with dizzy intensity, and more than usual pain.

Now the world was going crazy and it was so hot that she thought she might panic or scream. An anaemic trail of smoke ascended from the hills.

They looked out at the sweating sea, the sun melting into it like an iced lemon. "Does everybody have to have a child?" he said. "Do we?"

Kora tried to think. On one plinth, a full house, joy, pain, the koala bodies of young children, their ballast weight.

On the other plinth, herself, in front of a flower shop, seeing her own reflection in the glass, with one hand stretched out to touch.

At the beach, they lifted up stones and saw hundreds of

creatures living just under the world's skin, below the level of light. The stones were warm and damp. They went back to the B&B where they moved across each other like tides and he scattered salt pearls.

Janine Vanishes

Song: *Sweet Jane*, covered by Cowboy Junkies

Janine sits on the park bench, lit by intense August sun, the heat as heavy as a duvet. The hem of her dress brushes her sandaled feet, which are dusty from passing cars. A blotch of purple veins blooms on her ankle like a tangled city map.

She is sitting under a Japanese maple tree, planted to commemorate peace in the aftermath of Hiroshima. In front of her, in the yellow light, a fountain tumbles and breaks.

As the water rises and falls she remembers the thoughtful face of a boy, about eighteen, she saw in the gallery that morning. His face as half–absent as the faces of saints in the paintings around him, he was sketching a sculpture of a man about to dive. His concentration as he drew, the delicate whorls of his ears in the electric light, and his eyelashes casting shadows on his cheekbones, all moved her deeply. He sank so fully into his drawing that she lost herself in watching him. As he left the room, the trance cleared from his face, and Janine felt a moment of bliss. As she remembers it the feeling blooms again in Janine's chest, bigger in retrospect, overwhelming. It takes root inside her just as the fountain peaks, and she vanishes into another dimension.

It's true, she leaves the earth behind. She sees only a flash, then a distorting spectral rain.

Two faces are watching her through the gleaming permeable barrier, like the inside of a kaleidoscope.

Wt hapend? one says.

W mayd t to strong, the other says.

O sht.

They goggle at her.

Cn sh see?

Ys.

They're making an anxious low humming noise like the drone of huge bees. Their eyes shine like iridescent bowling balls. They seem embarrassed.

Janine floats, spaced out as a baby inside its caul. Nothing bothers her. This new dimension shifts dizzyingly. She smiles, stretching one hand out through the watery air, and they draw back with a buzz of shock.

Wat d w d? Mayk hir forgt?

... N. Dangris.

...... Snd hir bak?

......Ys. ......S ok.

The light shifts and dims then one, tilting to one side, says:
Wayt.

They push something round, buoyant, warm and yielding into Janine's hands. **Tak thys. Gft. Svenir.**

The pressure in Janine's ears breaks and implodes in black. She is sitting in the park just as before, but now she is holding a huge fluorescent balloon.

She winds the balloon's white ribbon around her wrist and keeps glancing up at it as she walks back to work for her afternoon shift. Bobbing serenely over her head, it looks like Jupiter. The light refracts around it, as if it has its own climate. Unlike most balloons, this is a perfect sphere.

Work doesn't feel so dull with the balloon floating over her. Janine sits in her chair at the corner of the gallery, gazing up at the balloon. Strangers smile at her in a gentle, humouring way. She smiles back at them. Many stop to watch her, thinking that she is an art installation, and film her on their phones, waiting for something to happen. The balloon bobs self–sufficiently beneath the ceiling of the gallery, which is painted in illusory clouds.

That evening Janine eats her lasagna–for–one with the balloon still suspended over her head. She scrolls through the news. Fires out of control in California. Seven Signs You Might Be A Psychopath. Donate to Save Coral Reefs. Man stalks and murders journalist, 21.

Janine glances at the balloon. Its glow must be clearly visible through the windows. She tries looking at it from various angles, its light hypnotic as a flame. Of course, it draws everyone's eyes towards it. She starts to feel afraid.

On reflection, she moves the balloon into a cupboard, where it will be safe. Whenever she opens the door, there it is, just as bright. She opens and closes the door a few times to make sure that it's still there. Then she leaves her flat.

Without a plan, she gets on the underground to Leicester Square. A man is sitting opposite her on the train with his head sunk in his hands. Janine's eyes rest on him as she idly circles one wrist with her other hand, still feeling the impression of the balloon's ribbon, which has left a static trace on her skin. As the train shrieks on the tracks the man looks up. The pain in his eyes is so jagged that she flinches as though hit. He looks back down at his feet.

Shaking, Janine gets out at the next stop, enters the nearest café and buys a tall caramel latte, sickly sweet.

She seems to have lost a layer of skin.

After the long glow of the afternoon, the world is steadily darkening, gaining a crayon–thick halo of black.

The café staff are playing a love song, in a slow, dreamy woman's voice. It swoons over her head. Janine is crying; people nearby look away, but one man keeps looking over at her. He has a burly sensitive face. She sees him through her tears, lifting his eyebrows apologetically. He gets up and offers her a paper napkin. Janine sobs, then starts to laugh. He sits down opposite her.

Later, they leave the café and go into a bar.

By the time they leave the bar, summer heat has broken into a downpour, turning them shiny and wet as otters. Rain gives a celluloid flicker to the air and streams through the dirt; its scent makes the city seem like it's growing out of the earth.

At the station, they watch a mouse foraging under the train tracks. Janine's hair drips down her back and she wrings out the hem of her dress. The mouse darts out of sight.

"The nerve they have," Fred says admiringly, then reaches down and wipes the rain from Janine's forehead. His eyes crinkle up with smile lines. "Sweet Jane."

As summer turns into autumn Fred and Janine walk together into lengthening nights. They hide indoors, sheltering against the weather, which is getting more extreme.

Each sunset feels increasingly unlikely, spilling rainbow cocktails across the smoky horizon as though to compensate for some encroaching threat. One night the sky turns every shade of red. The clouds are burnished copper.

Janine thinks about the co–existence of beauty and death, each clinging parasitically to the other. Personal feelings such as happiness or love seem to her like lit globes, substantial as air, in a brewing storm. She twines her fingers round Fred's wrist to stop herself from floating away.

The following spring, as Fred pushes his piles of boxes into Janine's flat, he opens the cupboard between the kitchen and the sitting room, and the balloon beams out with eager intensity.

"Jane? What's this?"

Janine stands beside him and they gaze at the balloon. It hasn't deflated one inch. Fred peers closer, mystified by the rhapsodic light scoring itself into its surface.

"Oh," Janine says. Her hand creeps to her collarbone, then

away. "That's mine. It was a gift. I'm keeping it in here — if that's okay."

Fred looks from Janine to the balloon. He smiles, perplexed. "Okay," he says.

Janine closes the cupboard door and leans lightly against his shoulder.

Circe

Song: *Sweet Dreams (Are Made of This)* by Eurythmics

That August noon, the sea barely seemed to move. Its dark blue silk looked ironed flat. In the pub garden, Claire loaded the creamy remains of Eton Messes onto her tray. Wasps nuzzled into cracked meringues and darted around her wrists, their dangerous barbed bodies specked with icing sugar, somehow embarrassed.

Inside the kitchen, the air sweated a heady mix of testosterone and grease. The chefs were all men, rankling in the swollen heat. The waitresses bobbed in and out, carrying loaded trays, entering the room backwards or kicking the door open with their feet.

"They said it was limp. They said they wanted a crisp, fresh salad," Claire said.

"Fucking bastards," Florin said. "Limp! Fuck off. I give them fucking crisps."

He arranged florets of fresh green leaves on the plate, muttering bitterly.

The staff were unexpectedly unwatched. Their boss, Delilah, had received sudden bad news that morning, and had left the pub, upset, in the chefs' hot hands.

Under pressure, Florin's rivalry with the head chef, Gabe, reached boiling pitch. Claire didn't know why they hated each other so much, with an intensity so pure it was almost lust. They screamed at each other until Gabe began grabbing pan lids from the rack and hurling them at Florin, who dodged.

Gabe was wiry and muscular, remote and unreadable, except for when he was angry. Florin had boyish features, though the hair around his temples was flecked with white.

One of the waitresses, Shona, was trying to intervene. She stood in front of Gabe in crab stance saying "wo, wo," as though she was trying to tame a wild animal. Gabe's face stayed stonily fixed on Florin's.

Florin caught Claire's eye from across the room. "He is a baby! He is a pig!" he shouted. "He's a baby's shit!"

Claire put her hands over her mouth to hide her laugh, and the edge of a smile crossed Florin's lips. After that they couldn't keep it up. Smiling ruined the self-seriousness that is necessary for violence to maintain itself. The fight died down as quickly as it had begun. Claire's t-shirt was damp and musty with sweat. She took a piece of ice from behind the bar and held it against the back of her neck, letting it melt between her shoulderblades. Work was slick with contact, from the sticky, meat–hewn bones on the plates, to the desires that steamed their way through the kitchen, leaving handprints on everything.

Shona was seventeen, vivacious and efficient, with an upturned, freckled nose, a wave of glossy hair tied back, down to her waist, and an attitude of barely held impatience. The chefs' gazes followed her across the room like insects crowding a goblet flower. Gabe, Grillo and Chris gathered around Shona as she put one arm round Gabe's neck and kissed his cheek. He grinned at the other men. She looked triumphant, surrounded by the triple halo of their attention.

Mali was watching Shona. Her husband, Kiet, worked beside her. When she stretched, he stroked her back. Mali glanced at Claire and shook her head, leaning confidingly over the counter.

"Shona should be careful," she said. "She doesn't know what they say at night, after work. It's disgusting."

Behind Mali, Kiet was watching the men, his eyes serious. Claire scraped ribs into the bin.

"Claire! You eighteen yet?" Grillo called.

"Yes," Claire replied.

"You should do porn," he laughed, and Chris whooped beside him. "Light it up!"

Grillo was called Grillo because he manned the grill. His

eyes had no warmth anywhere inside them and shone like the backs of cockroaches. Chris was young and slight, with a nervous, surreptitious face. His laughter echoed that of the older men, just a beat behind.

When Claire's break came, Florin said "You hungry? I'll make you something. On the house."

"Really?"

"Of course, darling."

Claire sat on the terrace eating the pasta Florin had made. It was 3pm. The horizon was getting heavy and grey, a warm wind starting to blow over the sea. From every window of the pub you could see it, ever–changing, the shadows of clouds lurking on its surface.

Florin came out for a cigarette.

"Soon, I'm getting out of here," he said. "Nothing happens. Boring."

"Where would you go?" Claire asked.

"Miami. Good clubs, parties all night, good times," Florin said, dancing. "Also, my son is there. He is thirteen."

"Aw."

"He hates me. His mother does too. She blamed me for the divorce." He exhaled smoke and flicked glowing ash on the terrace. "When I was young, I was angry. Very impatient. Not a good husband. Always arguing."

"But now," Claire said, "you're a saint."

Florin laughed. "If I move to Miami, maybe my son will love me again."

"He probably loves you, even if he doesn't like you."

"You are smart," Florin said.

"The pasta is good."

"Come to Miami, I'll make you fat."

Claire laughed.

"I'll take you to Miami, Claire. We'll dance all night."

Claire shook her head. She felt motherly towards Florin, though he was twice her age.

Shona was rolling cutlery. Claire stood alongside and started rolling too. "All right?" she asked.

"All right," Shona replied, circumspect.

Rolling cutlery was soothing, like putting dolls to bed. To make the napkins stick in a neat roll, they dipped the corner of them in water. They rolled and dipped, rolled and dipped.

"Does Grillo scare you?" Claire asked.

"Grillo? He's just a dickhead."

The corner of Claire's napkin had torn; she started again. "He scares me," she said.

Shona had finished rolling. "Posh girls," she said, "scare easily." She smiled and flicked a dishcloth at Claire then slipped back into the yellow light of the kitchen.

"I'm not that posh," Claire muttered.

As Claire carried a heavy tray of steak and chips into the garden, a huge dalmatian dog bounded towards her and she dropped the entire tray of food, gravy splattering the terrace. The dalmatian seized a rare steak and chewed, his white muzzle staining red.

"Ringo! Manners," the owner said. She was an elegant, coiffed woman in her sixties, fanning herself with a newspaper.

Florin, smoking on the terrace, had seen the crash. "Why is your dog free?" he demanded.

"We don't *tether* him," his owner said.

Florin took a deep breath and Claire saw the glee rising on his face. "Here, use this," she said quickly, taking off her work apron and tying it around the dog's collar, leashing him. His tail swished against her legs. "It's ok," she said to Florin.

"Oh no, it's going to rain," the customer said, glancing at the horizon. She held the dalmatian's makeshift leash in one limp hand, watching with mild interest as Claire and Florin cleaned slippery brown gravy off the terrace. Florin swept the broken plates into a large dustpan and silently handed it to Claire.

"I'm sorry," Claire said. She expected him to rant, but he just shook his head, returned to the kitchen and ordered three more steaks. She fetched a new apron and knotted it around her waist.

It was 6pm and the end of her shift when, patting her empty apron pockets, Claire understood that she had given her car keys to the dalmatian. The dog, his owner, and her original apron had all disappeared without a trace.

"Motherfucker. They'll be back," Florin said. "If you wait, I'll give you a lift when I finish."

"It's ok," Claire said. "I can make my own way." It would be a long walk home, but she wanted to get out of the pub and its heat.

The air was full of tiny thunder–bugs which stuck and writhed on her skin. The sea had turned grey and thick, dark clouds massing and rising over it after days of humid stillness. Claire felt the storm coming. As its light roiled and broke, she laughed with relief. The rain combed over the cliffs towards her, over her head, sluicing through her hair and trickling into her shoes.

The road home ran rigidly along the coast. She had been walking for some time and was soaked through when a car slid past, then abruptly pulled in and waited. The door opened and Florin waved.

"Get in!" he shouted.

As Claire slid into the passenger seat, dripping, she noticed Shona, who was sitting in the back like a child.

"All right," Shona said. She looked pale.

"I'm taking Shona home," Florin said. "A bad day."

"What happened?" Claire asked.

"Grillo, Chris and Gabe trap her in the storeroom," he said. He drummed his fingers on the wheel awkwardly. "I have to tell Delilah."

"Am I fired?" Shona asked in a tense voice.

"What? No, darling," Florin said.

Shona looked out of the window. Her mouth twisted and she pressed it firmly shut. Gobs of rain thudded on the windscreen.

"Hey. You want to watch the storm?" Florin asked.

He parked by the cliff, and they opened the doors to let fresh air in. Lightning was flickering over the water like lizard tongues, soundlessly, with thunder lagging behind. The smell of wet sand was rising all around them.

As the storm eased, Shona got out and stood on the cliff, stretching her arms out. Claire got out of the car and stood beside her. They looked at the changing colour of the water as the rain started to clear.

Claire looked at Shona. Her face was withdrawn, thinking. "I liked Gabe," she said. "Thought he was sweet."

Claire took her hand, then, just as quickly, let go. She didn't know if Shona wanted to be touched. Shona gave a short, muffled ha, between amusement and pain.

After they'd dropped Shona home, Florin drove deliberately fast, glancing at Claire and laughing whenever he took a bend. Claire clung tightly to the door handle, her wet clothes sticking to her skin.

Florin pulled up at the end of her drive, and the car engine lowered to a hum.

"Ok?" he said. "You are quiet."

Claire listened to the pressure of the engine. "Why did they do that?" she asked.

"To Shona?" He looked at her, turned the key, and the car throttled silent. "They are pigs. Listen darling, don't worry. Shit happens. You are young. Enjoy your life."

He looked out at the wet, shining road, then slammed one fist on the dashboard so hard that Claire jumped. "One day," he said, "I'll get to Miami. Then all of this will be just blue sky."

That night, Claire saw Shona standing in the pub garden in the dark. She was turning Grillo into a wild boar.

Does he scare you? Shona asked, stroking the tufts of wiry fur on his head, his teeth twisting slowly into yellowed tusks. Gabe was sniffing around her feet, whining. *Poor baby,* Shona said. Claire didn't know where Chris was, but something was chattering in the undergrowth behind them.

Claire dropped on to four paws, and backed into a tree. The branches were tangling over her and Florin was crouching in front of her, dropping treats. *Claire, come out,* he whispered. *I'll take you to Miami.*

As she woke, she heard an owl screech.

Peeling Oranges

Song: *I Put A Spell On You* by Screamin' Jay Hawkins

Brid dug her thumb into the skin of the orange, pulling the thick peel away in clumps like old wallpaper. She couldn't remove the tender inner layer stuck to the flesh, but she scraped at the fluffy white pith until a small wound appeared in the skin, the juice stinging. Almost nothing.

Unpeeled oranges sat on the kitchen counter, their colour intensifying the warmth in the room, which seemed to watch Brid and hold her in its light.

Brid had lived in London alone for nearly a year, on the top floor of an ex–council block. Ants invaded the kitchen, her tabby cat watching them with large green contracting eyes. Brid had given up trying to stop them. Take it, she thought, watching a winged soldier stagger away with a crumb. Roses splayed against the open window.

Sometimes after a long silence, her chest hurt, and she went out and sat in cafés, looking at other people until they got uncomfortable and moved away.

She had thought moving would make her feel new and full of possibilities, but her sense of strangeness was worse here than at home.

Today, though, she was going to Helene's housewarming.

Helene and Brid worked together in the library. Facing different walls, lit by bluely humming bulbs, they looked like opposites. Brid was small, plump, nervous and fluttery, with cheeks that flushed easily, and a pointed face like a hedgehog's. Helene was tall, dark, reserved, carefully detached. She spoke like a doctor examining a patient. Their brief conversations skimmed over light surfaces and vanished. Helene, Brid knew, had only invited her to be kind.

The sharp scent of oranges mingled with bittersweet chocolate. It wasn't necessary to flay it, but Brid was caught on the last bit of pith. Her mother once told her, always bring food when you go into another person's house. It'll stop you from getting under their skin.

She squeezed the naked, bleeding fruit into the bowl, then washed the sticky juice off her hands, rolled the truffles into small powdery balls, and put them in the fridge.

At work she wore white shirts and brown skirts which made her legs look chopped off at the calves. For the party she had bought an amber dress that clung too eagerly to her soft body. She put lipstick on and practised smiling, clownlike, at the mirror, then lay down, counting her breaths. She could hear a radio in another flat playing a slow song. South London stood in the August haze, saturated and steaming. Brid waited for the chocolates to set. She slept.

In the lengthening evening light, she took the chocolates from the fridge, put them carefully in a white cardboard box, tied it in a red bow, and left the flat still confused by sleep. The bus to Helene's house was crowded with hot bodies that crushed Brid damply against the window. She held the chocolates up, trying to keep them clear, but heard them rattling inside. Her hair stuck to her face and, when she looked, the chocolates were huddled in anxious clusters, like a clan of small animals, trailing cocoa. Her hands shook as she pulled them apart. Now her fingers were sticky. She wiped them, tried to smooth her hair and stood, sweating, at Helene's door.

"You made it!" Helene said, her voice politely bright.

Brid heard a cultivated bubble of voices and laughter. "I brought chocolates," she said.

"That's sweet of you. Where are they from? I'll put them in the fridge," Helene said tautly, without waiting for a reply. She sounded distracted. "I'll introduce you," she said.

She drew Brid across the room to two women who

seemed to know each other well, deep in conversation; their eyes flicked over Brid and quickly away. Helene had already vanished with a silky swish. Brid stood as far back from everybody as she could and scrolled stiffly through her phone. This place was loud with clinking glass and comfortable voices. Why was she here?

She moved back into the hall and pretended to look for the bathroom. A short dark–haired man was standing at the top of the stairs. "There's a queue," he said.

Brid stood awkwardly beside him, taking deep breaths. He glanced at her.

"We've not met. I'm Eric," he said, holding out his hand.

"Brid," she replied, shaking it.

Eric had a deliberately firm grip, and was forthright and curious, like a dog looking at a squirrel. His shortness, combined with his extreme confidence, was funny.

"That's an unusual name," Eric said.

Brid tried to breathe more casually. "It's short for Bridget. I don't like it. It reminds me of a horse."

Eric laughed, but in a kind way. Brid felt like a bud opened in her hand.

"Eric sounds like a Disney prince," she said. "In *The Little Mermaid*."

"Oh yes! Do you think I'm a good likeness?" He basked.

Brid was trying not to listen to someone pissing on the other side of the door. "I don't know," she said, embarrassed.

Eric was looking at her intently. "Brid," he said, "maybe you could help me."

The door opened with a loud flush. A stranger grinned broadly at them both and went downstairs.

"I want your input on something," Eric said, as if she was an employee. "Wait here."

He disappeared into the bathroom. Brid glanced down. She looked ridiculous in this dress, like a balloon animal.

Eric was washing his hands. He opened the door, stepped

out, and waited. "Aren't you going in?"

Brid hesitated, then told him that she just needed some space.

"You're hiding up here?"

"I'm not good at meeting people."

"You've just met me. How old are you? Twenty–five? Don't tell me. Old enough to know how to talk to people," Eric said. "Look. Let's have a chat, it's very safe."

He sat on the stairs and patted beside him. Brid sat down, trying not to laugh.

"I'd like your honest opinion on something. I'm a very good judge of people. I trust your judgement."

Eric was so open in his game–playing that it didn't feel like a trick. He was looking into her eyes. Brid tilted her head to one side and he lowered his voice confidingly. "There's a woman here, Josie, who I'm very attracted to. I don't know if her husband knows. I thought it was all in the open, but she's been ignoring me all evening. It's very frustrating!" He grinned.

"Oh," Brid said.

"Helene knows all about it," he said.

"Helene?"

Eric looked startled. "Yes, we're together."

"I didn't know."

"She's a very private person. Unlike me," he beamed. "I much prefer to be transparent. We'll all be *dead* in the end."

Brid nodded hesitantly. It was true. They would all be dead in the end.

"So," he said. "Should I speak to Josie about it?"

Brid struggled.

"I see. You're very conventional. Don't worry, let's go back down." Eric took Brid's hand and tugged her firmly after him.

"There you are," Helene said. She leaned into him like a gently blown tree, and Brid understood that she had never seen Helene relax before.

"I was getting to know Brid," Eric said.

"Good. Brid, have some champagne!" The glass fizzed in her hand.

"Brid, this is Josie," Eric was saying, steering her towards a pale, delicate–looking woman with her eyes heavily lined with black. "This is Clive."

Clive's face was serious and sleepy, but his dignity was wrecked by his hair, which swept off the top of his head as though in a strong wind.

"Brid, I will leave you with these *wonderful* people," Eric said. He kissed Brid's cheek and glanced at Josie, whose face showed the smallest flicker of pain. Clive didn't seem to notice.

"Eric, can you help me?" Helene called. He smiled like a Cheshire Cat and half–skipped across the room, sliding an arm round her waist.

Brid buried her nose in her glass.

"How do you know Eric?" Josie asked, forcing her eyes away from his back.

"I just met him," Brid said. "I work with Helene. How do you know him?"

"Life drawing."

"You're an artist?"

"No – I'm the model. It's quite tiring. I meet artists for interviews and it's very professional, but all the time they're trying to guess what you look like naked. The pay's okay, though. You should try it."

"Oh, I'd be no good."

"I'm sure you'd be *very* good," Josie said, with a slight smile. "Anyway, anyone can take their clothes off. It's easy. That's what Clive says."

Clive frowned.

"I think we need wine," Josie said.

Brid kept emptying her glass, and it kept refilling, thanks to Josie. Brid gazed at all the freckles on her cheekbones, gold and cream, like a woman in a Klimt painting. Then Josie swayed away on her platform shoes and Brid forgot to stop talking.

Clive seemed relieved not to have to say anything, inclining his head and intoning "Ah" like a priest, his expression far away. She had been quiet for too long. Now she couldn't stop confessing.

"But whataboutyour family?" she asked. She put a hand on his elbow to steady herself. He looked at it like it was a stick insect.

"We moved around a lot. My father was in the army."

"That sounds lonely," Brid said.

"I didn't really think about it. There was my sister."

"Areyouuuclose?"

"We never had very much in common."

"That'ssso sad," Brid said. Her eyes widened into Os.

Clive frowned into his glass.

"I wasssso lonely assachild," Brid said. "Weren'tyooou lonely?"

"That's an emotional way of putting it," Clive said. "I suppose so…" His gaze paled into the distance.

He's sad, Brid thought. I've made him sad. "'Scuse me," she said. The room was suffocating.

In the bathroom she splashed her face with cold water and sat with her head on her knees. She would have to stay up here. Hiding, as Eric said.

She crept into an empty bedroom, closed the curtains and sat on the floor, leaning her head against the wall, and closed her eyes. She would wait for it to end.

***

Then slowly, fringed by dim light, she heard muffled noises and movement, like the movement of midnight corals, late, and she opened her eyes to see Josie lying on the bed with her blue dress pushed up in waves, and Eric's face, strangely tender and self–satisfied, with one of his hands supporting the back of Josie's head. Brid saw her back arch and his other hand on the small of it, the last slant of sun through curtains, the fuzz of hair down his belly, Josie's feet against his chest, he was pulling Josie's dress down over her breasts, moving inside her until she gasped, and she hardly moved or breathed until Eric looked directly at her and he shouted and hit his head on the bedside lamp springing red with blood and he and Josie separated like scalded cats and Josie shrieked and scrambled under the covers and Brid tried to form an apology and Eric was just starting to laugh, when Helene's face, blank with certainty, loomed through the opening door.

"What's going on," Helene said. It wasn't a question. Eric was suddenly serious, trying to calm Josie by stroking her hair. She pushed his hand away; it had blood on it. He told Helene to go back downstairs.

Helene said that this was her room and she would not.

Josie fled past Brid, stumbling, and Brid backed unsteadily down the stairs, leaning against the wall. She heard Eric's lowered mumbling; the words NOT IN MY BED floated down the stairs, something broke against the wall and Eric fled past, with a quick shrugging glance at Brid. The front door slammed shut and the party hushed for a moment before the bubble of voices surged up again.

Helene emerged from her room and sat statuesquely on the top step with her feet neatly together, and a stone face. Brid asked if there was anything she could do. Helene huffed a short angry laugh. "I just want everyone to go away."

"Um. Hello," Brid said. She cleared her throat. A couple sharing a plate between them eyed her suspiciously. She had that inner shame, waiting for permission to exist, that invites only pity or contempt. She flushed, then tiptoed through the kitchen waste: branches stripped of grapes, rinds of baked brie like molten rocks, empty encrusted glasses of port, stale gin, cigarette stubs crumpled on white plates, spewing ash. She put the kettle on.

"I couldn't get them to leave," Brid said. "I made you some tea."

Helene was standing at the bedroom window, beneath which the lamp lay shattered into jagged moons. It had been thrown against the wall. Brid stood beside her, warm cup in one hand.

Josie was sitting on the pavement at the front of the house, sobbing noisily. "Cry me a river," Helene muttered.

Clive looked at a loss, then walked stiffly away. Josie trailed behind him, still crying.

Brid felt obscurely guilty.

Eric stood by the garden path looking after them, then turned and glanced up at the window. Helene opened it. "Go *away*! I don't want to see you!"

He too trailed off.

Helene let out a long breath. "He's such a shit."

"I'm sorry," Brid said.

"I don't know what you're apologising for," Helene said, then held her gaze for a knowing moment. She sipped her tea. "What were you doing in my room?"

"I drank too much. I had to sit down," Brid said. "Do you think you'll see him again?"

Helene took another sip. "Probably. I love him." She watched steam rising from her mug. Her quietness had controlled emotion inside it. "My dad kept all his affairs secret, you know. He lied *constantly*. I thought – I'm not being like them. I mean, he's right, it's best not to be. I was trying not to be."

Brid heard the unfamiliar appeal in her voice. "You deserve to be happy," she said blandly.

"Do I?" Helene smiled tightly. She looked at the time. "Oh… it's so late – you should head home. I'm sorry about all this. I'll see everyone out."

Brid was surprised when, at the door, Helene hugged her with unusual warmth.

Brid was sitting, still unsteady, at the bus stop, when Eric emerged from the shade beyond the streetlamps. The blood on his forehead had run into a spidery shape. He was trying to stop it with his hand.

"How is she?" he asked. He looked uneasy and out of his habitat. Brid saw that he didn't have anywhere to go. "Angry," she said.

He sat beside her, groaned and put his head in his hands. This wasn't what he had meant to happen, not at all. He wanted, very much, to make people happy. "I do! Really! I made Helene happy. I wanted to make Josie happy, too. She was lonely. Giving people what they want, if they're honest about it. Is that so bad?" He took Brid's hand. His breath grazed her cheek.

Brid looked into the growing shade of the trees. She thought that all her life, her love hadn't meant anything to anyone. She didn't know what to do with it. It was always a mistake, or in the wrong place, but it kept being there anyway, like the sun.

She stood up; the bus was coming. She pressed Eric's hand. "You're so lucky," she said.

The bus pulled away, leaving Eric sitting under the streetlamp, its light pooling around him. A drop of humid rain fell, and he looked up.

Brid gazed out of the window at strangers' faces bleached pale green in takeaway windows, strangers putting up their hoods and running down the street. Remembering Eric and Josie's surprised faces she started to laugh. A tired child, carried in her mother's arms, watched her solemnly.

Back in her flat, Brid listened to distant traffic and the rain on the roof as midnight spun into early morning. The night was full of people she didn't know. She felt as though they were all lying beside her in the dark. She imagined Eric trailing back to Helene's house and knocking on her door, or spending all night under the dripping trees, the rain mingling with his blood.

At the back of Helene's fridge, the chocolates sat in their box, full of oranges that grew in a tangled web of jewelled branches. When winter comes, Brid thought, the oranges will freeze solid, then they'll fall, smashing their shells of ice. She tried to gather them in her arms, but there were too many of them. They were too heavy, and her arms were tired now. All that fruit falling unseen —

she rolled over and fell asleep.

Sunita

Song: *Falling* by Haim

Maeve's friend Sunita died after a long illness. Maeve found it hard to admit that the news of her death felt like a broken shaft with a bird moving inside it. It was too transcendent an image for the messy pain that followed, but for a few seconds, the passage out of the world felt just the same as the passage into it. A closed circuit.

She chose not to see the body, thinking that husk might efface Sunita's whole life, blowing it away in dry dust.

For some time she compulsively imagined the moments before Sunita's death, but could only see a lone figure silhouetted at a window.

She became preoccupied with saving bits of Sunita for preservation.

Her smile was the salient point around which her face arranged itself, her large dark eyes like the pattern on a butterfly's wings.

The woodsy quality in her voice reminded Maeve of a clarinet.

She liked horror films and watched them in hospital in the middle of the night.

She was clear–eyed about the fact that, in her twenties, she was old before her time. She was angry.

The space of her illness felt teenage, only without any forward motion. Days passed in suspense. They watched music videos in her dad's sitting room, the coffee table covered in small rattling pill–bottles, orange and red.

Maeve slept over and listened to Sunita's light breaths. Death was very close, over their faces, like a giant hand.

It was impossible to describe a person after the fact. You had to see them to know them, absorbing their gestures.

Maeve tried again.

Sunita was warm, practical. She liked cooking.

Sunita loved Jarvis Cocker. A few years after her death Maeve happened to pass him on a London escalator. His beard was grizzled, half–covering his face, but it was him. He was going up; she was going down, into the underground. Maeve shouted "Hey, my friend loved you!" but he didn't turn around.

Sunita's dad spilled over with rage against everything that failed to save her, and Maeve saw that love could lie inside hate. It gave him something to do with his pain.

When Sunita died it was autumn, just starting to crisp with cold. The day was heavy and grey. Maeve turned on her electric heater and an admiral butterfly, asleep since summer, floated up. It looked hallucinatory, but it was alive. Maeve opened the window and watched it pulse into November on singed orange wings.

Anemone Hearts

Song: *Avant Gardener* by Courtney Barnett

–Did you know that if you cut a sea anemone into pieces, Maeve typed, –each part grows into a whole new anemone?

–Like plant cuttings.

–Yeah. They're going to use them for heart regeneration.

–That's interesting.

He sent an image of his heart medication.

–They make it heart–shaped, like I'm a child.

–How IS your heart?

–Ok, I think. I still have one.

Maeve looked out of the window. It had been raining. Now the rain had stopped and the pink hydrangeas outside looked golden in the late sun.

–Heart attacks sound scary.

–Yes. But if I died, I wouldn't care about it. I'd just be dead.

They worked together at the museum. He studied insects. He sometimes sat in the staff room with a giant stick insect climbing up his chest like a long baby. He handled cockroaches matter–of–factly, their bodies shining like swamp jewels. This lack of fear taught her something.

Once he took her to see a giant squid at the back of the museum. It was much more ordinary than she expected, blanched inside a narrow tank of preserving spirits. Nothing so miraculous as life.

She weighed the idea that a small piece of an organism could hold the whole, or that death could simply be discarded from consideration, in favour of presence, staying on the map.

Maeve liked to hold every thread.

Sometimes friends dropped each other casually, especially when they fell in love or had children. They outgrew people,

people outgrew them. It happened and they didn't even sound upset. She didn't understand it yet; the land kept spreading and diverging around her. She hardly let anyone go by choice.

She sent him phosphorescent sea creatures.

He sent her peacock caterpillars, black and thorned, silhouetted against white sky.

BUDDIES

Songs:

Roller Girl by Anna Karina

Oh Bondage! Up Yours! by X–Ray Spex

My bed was full of flowers. A lily the colour of an opened nectarine was crushed against my ear, and bees hummed like voices through a door. My hands were half–clenched; I blinked and the sun turned neon.

I crept downstairs. The kitchen went silent as I entered the room, the air full of an imminent fight. Mum was making coffee, looking tired. Dad sulked at the table, his breakfast softening in the bowl. Nan sat silently in her armchair by the window; I rolled my eyes at her. She smiled sadly back. Since her stroke, she didn't talk, except with her eyes.

This kitchen mood left no space to stop for anything more than emergency supplies, so I put an apple and a chocolate bar into my bag and retreated upstairs to shower. Something smashed downstairs. I hummed and turned the water as hot I could, nearly burning, watching steam billow against the door. I brushed my teeth too hard and spat out some blood, pink in the froth.

When I returned to my room the flowers were still there, shiny and translucent. I was relieved. You and me, buddies. I nodded at them and pulled a brush through my hair. The shower had left red patches on my shoulders where the water touched them, like demon handprints.

In Sixth Form no–one can tell you what to wear. I pulled on a yellow dress like a highlighter pen, a long black cardigan, daubed eyeliner around my eyes, then blotted it so it didn't smudge.

When I came downstairs Mum was sweeping broken glass with a dustpan and brush. She had cut one of her hands and a few drops of her blood were smeared on the tiles. I knew not to ask, the same way you don't ask when you pass an ambulance in the road, you just walk by. I took the dustpan from her and swept up the rest of the glass as she hovered anxiously. "Clumsy," she murmured. Dad's hands were taut on the edge of the table. Nan looked upset.

I threw my hands up in defeat. "See you later," I said.

It was spring and the birds were going insane. I hopped over puddles towards the bus stop. David was there before me. He had only joined the school recently, but I already liked the soft edges of his jumpers, his lightning–bolt shirts, and his look of relief when he recognised me. I lifted one hand for a high five and he held it instead, then let go. He asked how my continued existence and one life on the planet was going for me, and I told him that my parents were fighting again. David said that sucked. I told him that it was stupid, but it didn't matter. I put my hand to my forehead then lifted it away. "See? It's gone."

David was looking closely at me. "I had a bad morning too," he said. "My dog ran away."

"Oh no," I said.

He had an unusual expression that I couldn't place. He said that his dog had run down the street chasing after a car. Did I want to help him look for her?

I asked his dog's name.

"Kazoo."

"I didn't know you had a dog."

"Yeah. She's a mongrel."

"I hope we find her."

"After school, we'll look for her."

The bus pulled up, screeching. We both flinched and nearly touched but did not.

All day I thought about Kazoo chasing the car, barking manically, her padded feet skittering on the hard road.

The great thing about cars, I thought, from a dog's point of view, was that you could never catch them. They flew into hope and the future that you can't see.

My friend Sadie nudged me and whispered, "you look happy."

I met David by the school gates. He was carrying two ice creams, one of which he was eating. The other was melting. "Please say you like chocolate," he said.

I confirmed that I did.

He said we had to go to his house to get the MISSING posters, and was that okay? I nodded, eating the ice cream quickly to catch the drips, then chewed up the last of the cone. My teeth ached. The blossom was soft and crunchy under our feet. David looked nervous. We were at the end of the street when he turned and said quickly, "I don't really have a dog."

He explained that he did have a dog once, and she was called Kazoo, and she did run out after a car, but it was years ago, and she had never returned.

I told him that this was a shocking lie to tell me, an innocent. I'd been thinking about that dog all day. Now she turned out to be no more than a non–dog running down the road after the skeleton horse of Death.

"I'm sorry," David said. He took my hand. "I just wanted a stupid reason to ask you out. Is that okay?"

We looked at each other and the space between us was a terrifying abyss. When I kissed him our lips were cold from the ice.

I told David never to lie to me again, and he said, recklessly, that he would not.

David's house was small like mine but it felt comfortable inside, as though one of his soft jumpers had stretched into house form. His little sister, Dot, was lounging on the sofa. She had bright curious eyes and reminded me of a harvest mouse.

"Hi Dot. This is Julia."

"Hi." Dot scrutinised me. "How old are you? I'm ten."

"I'm seventeen," I said, smiling.

"Where are mum and dad?" David asked.

"They went to the beach."

They had left a note saying GONE TO THE SEA BACK LATE HELP YOURSELF xxx

"That means they're at the pub," David said.

"Can I sleep at Bella's?" Dot asked.

"As long as her parents don't mind."

"It's fine. She asked them already." Dot went to her room and started packing a flowery rucksack.

"Take a toothbrush, you animal," David said affectionately.

"Oh–kay" Dot said. Drawers clattered open and closed.

"Bella lives in a big house," David said. "Sometimes I think Dot wants to live there."

"They have nice food," Dot yelled. "And a swimming pool!"

"Oh, I see!" David shook his head at me in fake disapproval. "She's so mercenary."

"What's mercenary?" Dot asked. She was wearing her flowery rucksack and carrying a toy fox with frayed paws.

"It means you're cut–throat."

"Cool."

"It also means you're greedy."

"*Whut?'*

"Exactly," David said. "Have fun. Be polite."

"I'm polite!"

"Hmm."

After Dot had gone, David made us a meal that he called the Tower of Bagel. It was a stack of three bagels on top of each other, which he skewered together and then sliced in half. "I can't believe that Dot likes the food better at Bella's," he said solemnly.

I couldn't finish the Tower of Bagel. I swallowed and put the plate down. David reached across the small kitchen table and touched my face and I leaned into his hand, then he picked me up, his hands pushing up between my shoulder–

blades and half–carrying me into his room.

We lay on David's bed looking out of the window at the grey road. I stroked his eyebrows then turned flat on my back and said, "When I woke up this morning my bed was full of flowers."

"That's funny," he said. "Did you plant them there?"

"I must have," I said. 'They were growing like crazy."

Blue light was filtering through the window. It was getting dark. "You should call home," he said, "they'll wonder where you are. Do you want to stay over?"

"Yes." I watched car headlights move over the ceiling. "I want to chase cars with you," I said.

I called home and said that I was staying at a friend's house.

"At Sadie's?"

"No. At David's."

"Your friend from school?"

"It's fine. He's really nice. I'll see you tomorrow."

She sounded anxious so I assured her of my sound mind and good judgement.

I wondered whether the flowers were still in my room. I huddled against David's chest, but sleeping was awkward in his single bed, so we lay head to toe.

The front door opened and closed. We heard footsteps and muffled laughter.

"You can meet my parents in the morning," he murmured.

"Will they mind me staying?"

"They won't mind. They're very laid back."

During the night we woke up and kissed in a barely–there state. I'd never felt so awake.

It was Saturday. When David's parents got up, David was making breakfast and I was on the sofa, reading a book I had found on the shelf called *BY GRAND CENTRAL STATION I SAT DOWN AND WEPT*. David's mum was wearing a silky dressing gown and groaning.

"I made you eggs," David said. "This is Julia."

"Oh shit!" she said. "I didn't know we had a *guest.*"

She was disconcerted, then smiled radiantly. Her name was Liana. Her dark hair was piled high on her head and some eyeliner from the day before still clung around her eyes. She had a glamour so different from my mum's eggshell anxiety that I tried not to stare.

She stretched, hugged David and kissed his cheek. "Where's Dot?"

"She stayed at Bella's."

There was a bang and David's dad hopped into the room holding his foot, a red sarong tied around his waist. "Ow," he said.

"Jason, get dressed. David's friend Julia is here," Liana said.

"Bloody hell," Jason said. He disappeared into their room then re–appeared, buttoning his jeans. He had long hair and a tattoo of thorns circling his right wrist. "Who is this?"

"Julia," Liana said.

"Hello Julia."

"How was your swim?" David asked.

"Rubbish," he shuddered. "It was freezing, so we went to the pub."

David put plates of egg and toast in front of them.

"You're an angel," Liana said. "Isn't he an angel, Julia?"

We listened to the radio and drank coffee with sun streaming into the kitchen. It was Heaven. No one was fighting. Jason even looked like Jesus, with his long hair and the odd–shaped amulet around his neck.

"It's a wishbone," he said, seeing me looking at it. "David, where did you find this girl?"

"At school, where do you think?" Under the table, David squeezed my knee. I flushed and looked down at my book. Liana smiled kindly. "More coffee?"

I didn't want to go home, but I needed clean clothes. David

kissed me at the end of my street. "Should I come in with you?"

I said that wasn't a good idea. We agreed to meet at the cinema.

I slipped in and smiled through the doorway at Nan, who smiled faintly back. The house seemed quiet. I was moving towards the stairs when Dad said "Jules."

He was leaning against the kitchen counter with his back to me, like a Bond villain. He sounded angry. I watched him from the doorway.

"Come here," he said.

I stayed where I was. He turned around.

"I know what you've been doing," he said. "You're just like her."

I began to absent myself from the conversation, but he said, "I get home, she's not here, you're not here…"

"What?"

"She's gone."

I have my dad's eyes, like two dark marbles, and we gazed stonily at each other. I said that I didn't know where Mum was, but I hoped she was happy and far away, and all the worst things I could think of saying to him. Nan made a distressed sound. I ran upstairs and bolted the door of my room, which was now so crowded with wild plants I had to pull my clothes out of vines like strange tangled crops. Dad was thumping at the door. I opened the window and looked down. There was a drop, but the porch roof made it possible.

Now he wasn't shouting, but crying, which was worse. I crawled out of the window, through the tendrils, and jumped.

I met David at the cinema, where I changed my clothes and washed my scrapes. I cried in the toilet cubicle. A poppy poked over the edge of the stall, its centre a black eye. I wondered where Mum was. I'd tried calling, but her phone was off.

Sometimes when Dad was out I had overheard her talking on the phone in a low voice, laughing. I knew that was a secret without having to ask.

Of course, David said, I could stay with him. We were watching *Eternal Sunshine of the Spotless Mind*, he was moving his hand up my thigh, and I leaned into his neck trying not to make a sound.

Back at David's house Liana and Jason were very concerned. Of course, they said, of course I could stay. They were both flushed and couldn't stop laughing. Liana stroked my hair.

David rolled his eyes at me. "They're high."

"Shhh," Liana said, and giggled. "Stay as long as you like honey. As long as you need."

Jason lay on a pile of cushions, languid as a sunbathing lizard, his angular feet bare, his nails getting long. "Welcome home," he said, with a wry smile.

In bed, I murmured into David's chest, "How old are your parents?"

"Mum's thirty–four. Dad's thirty–seven. She was seventeen when they had me. Fifteen when they met."

"Wow."

"I take care of them."

"You're the grown up one," I said.

"I'm well responsible."

"That's sweet."

"Thanks." He was quiet. "I love them," he said, "but they're not, like, the most reliable people."

I moved so we were head to toe. I was trying to get used to sleeping next to someone else, but my body wouldn't rest. After David fell asleep, I listened to him breathing, feeling like a guard dog.

Sunday arrived, drizzling. David had to go to work at the Starling Café, where he had a weekend job. "I'm sure I could get you a shift," he said.

I said that would be good, that I needed a job. I thought of the chaos of my room, Nan's stricken face, the crying on the other side of the door. I told David I'd meet him at the café. I had to call my mum.

"Okay," he said, and kissed my cheekbone.

After he left, I called my mum's mobile. It rang and rang. When she picked up her voice sounded fuzzy and sad. She told me things abut herself and my dad that made my head hurt. I told her that I could take care of myself. She said she'd try to see me soon. No–one could know where she was. She said that there wasn't enough space for me there yet, but she would make space, and I could come and live with her as soon as there was space. A man's voice murmured in the background.

I had never thought that she might not have space. There had always been enough space for me wherever she was. I said, okay, keeping my voice steady.

"Are David's parents home? Can I talk to them?"

I listened; the house was still. "I don't know," I said. "I'll give them your number to call you back, okay?"

When I said goodbye my voice wobbled at the last moment. I hung up. "Shit," I muttered.

There was a quiet tap on the door. Jason asked if everything was all right.

I wiped my eyes, opened the door said in my most calm voice that everything was all right, but that I couldn't go home. Was it really okay for me to stay?

"Our pleasure," he said, padding through to the kitchen. "Can I make you a drink?"

I curled up on the sofa while he glugged ingredients together. I took a few sips. "Does this have alcohol?"

"Haven't you had a hot toddy before? There's not too much in there."

"It's nice, thanks."

"You're very welcome."

Sun slanted through drizzle on the window. "It's clearing up," I said.

Jason sat in the armchair opposite me, watching me with an amused expression. "Tell me about yourself. What do you like to do?"

I told him I was studying Art, Maths, History, and Film, and that I wanted to make films.

"You look like an arty girl."

"Thanks."

"Have you seen any Godard?"

"I've heard of him. I haven't watched his films."

He told me I looked like Godard's muse, and found an image of an actress called Anna Karina. "That's you."

I looked closer at the image, but didn't see myself in it. We had similar eyes, but my face was more round. She was wearing an orange shirt, stripy socks, and a motorbike helmet. "She looks happy," I said.

"Yes," he said. "She's very happy."

In the course of conversation, his voice had gradually turned husky and intimate, as if he was slowly stroking a rabbit's fur. The house felt very quiet.

"Where's Liana?" I asked.

"She teaches a pottery class on Sundays. You should go along, you'd enjoy it. Want a top up?"

I said no, I was feeling much better now. I asked if he would call my mum and wrote her number down on a scrap of paper.

"Of course," he said, taking it from my hand. "We'll take good care of you."

He stood over me for a moment. He smelled of pot and shampoo. I said that I had to meet David now.

"Lucky David," Jason said.

Sunday afternoons were busy at the café. At the end of his shift, I helped David dry plates. "Don't tell my boss," he said. "I'll buy you dinner." We flicked hot water at each other.

Afterwards we ate Chinese takeaway by the river. The lamps reflected in the water like chrysanthemums.

"This is the best weekend of my life," David said.

"We haven't lived that long."

"My life so far."

"What do you think we're going to do, for the rest of our lives?"

"I don't know. I hope it's interesting. I like writing stupid things."

"You never told me that."

"I wrote something for you, actually. Prepare yourself. *Julia, Julia, she's so cool–ia*."

"Oh my God."

"You're welcome."

When we got back to the house, David's parents were snoring, and Dot was fast asleep on the sofa, her shoes scattered on the floor. David got the duvet from her bed and draped it over her. "It's not worth waking her," he said.

When we got into bed, I saw a trail of white convolvulus flowers pressed against the window. They had followed me. I gazed up at their sheer snowy peaks until sleep came.

It was funny riding the bus to school with David with our hands twined together.

I told Sadie about Mum leaving, and Dad's meltdown, but not much about David. He was private. I was beginning to feel that other people could be a place to escape into.

That evening David had a shift at the café. He asked if I would hang out with Dot, as she was alone at home. Dot and I drew cartoons together and I answered her questions. What was my favourite colour? (Green.) What was my favourite animal? (Wombat.) What was my favourite food? (Ice cream.) What was my favourite letter of the alphabet? (X.) What was my favourite song? (*Oh Bondage! Up Yours!* By X Ray Spex).

"That's a lot of x's," Dot said.

"Yep," I said.

I found X Ray Spex on the internet and we were dancing when Liana and Jason got home. I turned the music off.

"Don't stop," Jason said.

"Is there any food?" Liana asked, opening the fridge. "Oh. No. Let's order takeaway."

We ate Indian food and watched *Manhattan* while Liana and Jason shared a joint.

I didn't feel comfortable sharing it with them but the fact that they offered it to me made me feel sophisticated. The smoke made me thirsty and heavy.

Dot didn't like the smell and said she was going back to Bella's house tomorrow. I wondered if I could go to Bella's house too. When there is not enough space for you in one house, you have to find other kinds of house. I was lucky that Jason and Liana were being so nice to me. Liana had fallen asleep against Jason, with her head on his shoulder. I was sitting on the floor next to the sofa when Jason began to stroke my hair with his free hand. "Beautiful," he said. All the hairs on my body prickled up in spikes. I slid over to the beanbag in the corner and curled up very tightly with my eyes closed. I stayed frozen there, until I heard Jason and Liana's breaths deepen into snores.

"Fuck's sake," David was saying. He was pulling Liana and Jason up from the sofa. "Go to your room!"

"Nooo," Liana said.

"Yessir," Jason said, winking at me. They trailed to their bedroom.

I felt blurry. "What time is it?"

"Late." David sounded annoyed. "Why do they have to be so…" he waved his hand, exasperated.

I nodded. I didn't mention Jason stroking my hair. It felt unmentionable.

The next day I ate breakfast in David's room, with the door shut. He opened it and peered around the door. "What are you doing in here?"

"Stay with me," I said.

At school I asked Sadie if I could stay with her that night.

"Did you and David fight already?"

I said no, it had just been three days. I didn't want to overstay.

"Shit. Are you homeless?"

I said, of course not.

"I think somebody should know if you're homeless."

"I have a home," I said, fiddling with a daisy chain I'd made around my neck. "I just can't live there."

When I told David I was staying at Sadie's, he said "Why?"

"Because I feel like it. I like Sadie. It'll be fun."

Sadie and I watched *Ten Things I Hate About You* and talked about starting a band. Neither of us had instruments or knew how to play them. "I'm going to save up," I said, and clapped my hands.

The next day I went straight from school to the Starling Café for my trial shift. David's boss, Yvonne, said that we shouldn't work the same shifts. We would distract each other, she said, pushing her glasses up her nose.

David sat patiently at one of the tables, supposedly doing homework, really watching me learn to make coffee, with a quiet attentive expression.

"Fine," Yvonne said, eventually. "If you're just going to *sit there*, do you want my shift?" She threw her apron at him.

I learned to froth the milk gently, so that it didn't bubble and shriek. Our backs and shoulders ached. We swept, mopped and cashed up.

David kissed my ears. "Are you staying at Sadie's again tonight?"

"I want to be with you," I said.

We ran through the park and crept into the bushes. "We could just stay here," I said, pressing my hands into the earth.

David put his hands over mine. We saw a frog crawling through leaves, its throat pulsing, its back like a glossy wet stone.

At David's house, everything was quiet. Jason, Liana and Dot were asleep. We rested.

Jason happened to be by the bathroom door when I came out of it the next morning, wrapped in a towel. I moved around him, apologising. I apologised very much, pulling my towel more tightly around me, and he watched me walk away.

"Why are you getting dressed under the covers?" David asked.

"I just feel like it," I said. The convolvulus was getting thick at the window.

"Coffee?" Liana asked. She always looked pretty and made up, even early in the morning. She had a sweet trusting face, and I didn't think she noticed Jason looking steadily at me, because she had her back to him. I tried to focus on my book, then David walked in and Jason looked out of the window. I drank my coffee too fast and scalded the back of my throat.

That evening we had no shifts. We went to the park and listened to music. It was peaceful there with just the two of us, and I didn't want to leave.

"Do you want to *live* out here?" David asked.

I had my back against a tree. "Maybe."

"You seem sad."

"I'm not," I said. I was happy, but also afraid.

When we got back, Jason, Liana and Dot were watching television.

"Join us," Jason said. "It's Godard."

"It's *bor*ing," Dot said.

Anna Karina was dancing, smiling, dancing. The men on either side of her were following the same pattern as she was, following her steps. Then she danced alone, laughing and looking at us, waiting for the camera to stop watching her. We stayed for a little while, sitting on cushions, until I felt Jason's foot press into the small of my back.

I said that I was tired and went to bed.

The next morning, I thought, I just won't shower today. I stayed wrapped in the sheets. "Are you feeling ok?" David asked.

I said that I missed my mum and started crying.

"Maybe you should stay here today," David said.

"No, I'm going to school with you."

I usually liked Maths, which had a system of understandable rules that I found reassuring, but it didn't seem capable of helping me today. I drew my mum's face, then drew flowers over her worry lines.

Sadie wrote on my arm *Are U OK*.

I asked if I could stay at her house that night.

"My aunt's visiting, so my sister's in my room. You could still come over?"

I said never mind, maybe another time.

During the break I called my mum and left a message on her voicemail asking if she was all right. I was totally fine, I said. I just really wanted to know if she was okay.

"If your dad's been calling her all the time, she probably turned her phone off," Sadie said.

"Probably," I said, scuffing my foot against the concrete.

When we got back to David's, Liana was out, teaching her yoga class. Jason wasn't home — which meant he was at the pub, David said — and Dot was at Bella's. The house was empty. We laughed to ourselves, and took a bottle of wine from the fridge. We sat with David's arms around my waist, watching *The Office*.

The phone rang. Dot was calling from Bella's house, where Bella had pushed her into the swimming pool. Dot was crying.

"I'll go get her," David said, "I'll be back soon." The door slammed shut behind him.

The house was silent then except for the quiet rustle of leaves at the window. I read more of *BY GRAND CENTRAL STATION I SAT DOWN AND WEPT*. It was supposed to be about love, but I wasn't so sure if that was the case. There didn't seem to be more than one person in it, only a single voice, insistent and unnerving.

The front door opened.

"How's the book?" Jason asked. His voice sounded normal, but I scanned my position. My feet were up against the coffee table, which he was standing on the other side of. My phone was charging on the other side of the room. I said that it was meant to be a love story, but I thought love should make a person happier than this book seemed to be.

Jason asked if love made me happy, then began to ask other, more disturbing questions. He was breathing heavily. I lifted my knees up to my chest. I had never shaken with fear before. One part of me shook while the other observed the shaking. I knew that Jason was starting to do something unacceptable, and also knew that I had run out of places to escape into; this realisation went on for longer than I wanted.

Then the convolvulus burst through the window.

The plants had been building up to this for days, in their collective mind, and their combined weight broke the frame all the way through. Glass and splintered wood shivered over the room and I screamed.

David, Dot and Liana were there now, Dot's wet hair framing her confused face; Liana was holding her hand.

Jason got up and let go of me. Dot ran to her room.

Jason said that I was a bit upset about my mum and dad. I was crying.

"Are they okay?" Liana said. Her gentle face looked perplexed by what she had just seen and seemed to be quickly and efficiently trying to erase it.

"No, no," David said. "I don't think that's it." I looked at David and he looked steadily back.

"I was comforting her," Jason said.

"He was comforting her!" Liana laughed anxiously.

David looked at me.

This was why, after the shouting and screaming and Dot saying she was going to run away to Bella's house, David and I were sitting on a park bench, watching the stars constellate, and the cold moon. David's face was still. The fabric of reality had changed. Changes don't settle easily on any familiar face, expressing intentions and actions incompatible with the person who was kind to us, or the person we loved. We had been living inside a wrong understanding of the world. We did not understand the things that people do.

The truth is, I'm not sure. My memory is patchy. I filled the holes in with new earth. Did the flowers burst through the window, or did I grow them there afterwards, so that I could tell this to you now?

I'm here, after all, to protect you.

The grass was studded with daisies, tightly closed. In the morning they would open again. All they needed was sun, soil and rain. David was saying that we would find our own place, though I wasn't sure where we would get the money. It didn't seem to matter. I was very tired. I rested my head on his lap. "Living the dream," I said.

"You and me, buddy. Chasing cars."

We both howled at the moon.

Red Kite Falling

Song: *Perfect Day Elise* by PJ Harvey

"Let's go look for Will and Elise," I said.

Francis was lying in dappled shade with his head in my lap. A leaf, parched and veined, had fallen in his hair. He yawned. "Why?"

I watched a child's red kite rise unsteadily overhead, then tumble suddenly down. "What else is there to do?"

Summer stretched out in blue tracts of time. The park was littered with smouldering barbecues and paper cups lined with sticky, idle sweetness.

Will and Elise had disappeared just before exams started. "Probably eloped," Francis had said, then laughed with an edge of jealousy.

Will and Elise often took off for a few days, but they had really vanished this time, no joke.

My romantic ideas about Will and Elise were stupid and I knew it. Their disappearance tugged at me. I couldn't imagine doing that, walking away.

Will moved dreamily, as though only the direct presence of others could force him to stay in the room, but I couldn't imagine Elise anywhere other than right here, right now.

She was cagey about her past, had no family photos on her wall, and never seemed to leave town until she met Will.

She was always dying her hair a brighter colour or trying a newer, better kind of exercise, or tightrope–walking down the halls. Francis sardonically called her a Manic Pixie Dream Girl.

I was always trying to sit closer to Elise.

How in love she and Will seemed, their bodies entwined and conspiratorial.

I wanted to feel like that. I felt dysfunctional, faulty.

I scrolled through Elise's social media. She hadn't posted anything since the last photo, by Will, of her silhouetted, with the sun behind her, her head thrown back, her arms out. Nothing around her but sky, no way of telling where she could be.

The photo was weeks old. They could be anywhere. I stroked Francis's hair, still scrolling with my other hand. "Where do you think they went?"

"I don't know," he said. "How about Scarborough."

I considered this. Elise did like the sea. She often posted photos of shells, upturned, in the sand, with their pink hollow insides exposed.

"Yeah," I said. "Why not. Let's look for them there."

"*She once was a true love of mine,*" Francis sang, and smiled winsomely up at me, his eyes shining like dark suns.

I saw a mosquito land on my arm. It steadied itself; soon it would start to drink. It unfurled its spindly proboscis. I decided not to brush it away. I watched it feed on me, its abdomen swelling with my blood, like a cursed fairy–light.

Francis was looking at me, expectant, then he sighed. "Okay," he said, "let's go!"

I liked this about Francis: he was adventurous. We ran over the grass.

On the train we drank bitter coffee in polystyrene cups. "Yeuch," Francis said, pulling a face. I stirred in a packet of sugar and began adjusting my taste buds.

Francis was plaiting my hair, which had grown long and tangled.

"You should curl it," he said. "It wouldn't take long. It'd look nice. I can curl it, I'd like that. You'd look really pretty."

"Yeah, okay."

"Also, you should wear more black."

I was wearing a turquoise dress. "Don't you like this?" I

asked.

"Black looks good on everyone," he said.

I fiddled with the bracelet on my wrist. The train rattled over the tracks.

"Hey, let's stay the night!" Francis exclaimed, as we wandered down the winding streets.

"Sure, okay," I said.

He twirled me around and kissed me.

I knew that this was romantic and that I was meant to respond accordingly, but with Francis I kept turning papery, decorative, watching myself from the outside, or being dragged along in his wake.

What was a personality, anyway? Just a stolen compilation of everyone you ever met. Maybe I could be this person, curl my hair, wear black. Francis was being nice to me, being fun, being the life and soul.

He was looking into a shop window. "Let's try on hats," he said.

The hat he brought me was wide–brimmed, green and looked like a hat from a film noire. It cost £80. "Why not?" he said. I put it on, smiled, posed.

Shopping trips with Francis were dizzying. We'd go out to buy milk and come back with three pineapples, baklava and Turkish delight. My life before I met him was comparatively ordinary. It felt like being a girl in a film.

At night he'd fall asleep holding my hand, looking sweet and defenceless. I felt my power over him, and did not want it.

We found a B&B to stay in that night and reserved a room. It had floral pillows and musty undertones of damp, muffled by lavender spray, genteel and elderly.

Francis sat on the bed and bounced. "Yay!" he said. "Let's go out!"

Down every street I looked for Elise, although I knew she wouldn't be here. Not really. Still my eye caught every change in the light.

We found a curry house and ate until we were full, drinking bottles of beer. Francis was animated and charming, making big plans, and I let myself get caught up, nodding in all the right places.

On the way back to the B&B, I felt sick. We were walking down the sea front when I leaned into the clammy wind, bent over and vomited. Francis was tender and attentive, stroking my back and hair.

In our room I felt sweaty and shivering, went into the bathroom, which was stomach-pink, and retched. The yellow, stringy curry burned in my throat.

I had a distinct sense that Francis was enjoying this opportunity. "I'll take care of you!" he exclaimed.

He went downstairs to request some peppermint tea, then watched me sip it slowly down.

"Thank you," I said.

He rested my head on his shoulder, stroked my hair. The room receded woozily.

"Francis," I murmured. "We need to break up."

"Shh. No, we don't," he said.

"We do. I'm sorry."

"You're tired. You don't mean that."

The light pixelated through my half–closed eyes.

"You'll feel better in the morning. We'll go to the beach. I love you," he said.

"You don't," I said. "I'm not even here."

"No, I love you," he said. He held me fast as I fell asleep.

That night I dreamed of Elise. She was wading through ivy, through nettles, getting stung, and I was following her. She seemed oblivious – I was translucent – then she suddenly turned, smiled, waved.

The next morning Francis and I peeled on our day–old clothes. We went to see the surf washing over the broad sands.

We passed old stately hotels, and the bay curved around us, pulling clouds down towards it. I could see rain coming, the sunlight a sulphurous yellow against the grey.

Francis spread out his jacket on the sand for me to sit on, then knelt down a few feet away and started digging a hole with his hands. "What are you making?" I asked.

"I don't know," he said. He kept going.

I watched the stubborn back of his head for a while, then looked away up the beach and thought, for a moment, that I saw Will and Elise. She was doing cartwheels at the edge of the foaming sea, and Will was photographing her. Then I saw that this Will was heavier, thicker–set, and this Elise had hair down to her waist, too long. It wasn't her.

I tried to read but the words were all pointless.

Francis had finished digging his hole and was sitting inside it like a puppy, looking at me with bright inquisitive eyes.

I pulled my phone out of my bag and scrolled restlessly. Elise's page was still silent.

Will's was blank, too. The last thing he'd shared was the image of Elise.

"Where did they *go*?" I said.

Francis had climbed out of his hole and was standing over me. Looking wistful, he held out a hand to help me to my feet. "They'll show up."

We were both quiet on the train, tired from wading in cold water. I leaned into Francis's shoulder, trying to feel comfortable, then opened my phone and searched for Elise.

Nothing came up. I searched again.

Will had posted something on his page. I was afraid to look at it. The fear ran through me without warning, all the way to the bone. My stomach hurt. "Elise?" I said, and felt love rise sickeningly through my chest.

Will

Song: *Heavy Water/I'd Rather Be Sleeping* by Grouper

The secure ward, like the inside of a sad Teletubby house. Patients shuffle out of their rooms in soft and harmless clothing. The furniture is all wedge–shaped, and the air smells of sweat.

Will is looking at Elise but Elise can't look at him. She picks at her sleeve then hides her face behind her hair and hand.

Heavy, heavy water.

Elise: "I'm so tired."

The Relaxation Room is painted with an underwater scene: clownfish, angelfish, octopus. The octopus is smiling and has wide white cartoon eyes. A purple jellyfish looms beside it.

Will: "You scared me so much I started talking to myself. In the lift up here, I was going fuck, fuck, shit…"

Elise: "I'm sorry. It's hard to explain."

Will: "How are you feeling?"

Elise: "I don't feel much at the moment. Not even love. I know I should feel it.… I know. I don't want to be here."

Will suppresses tears.

Elise (*pained*): "Please don't cry." (*She looks at the fish on the walls*). "It's just like, you're swimming in the water, you have gills, you can breathe. Then it pulls you in."

Will: "So it's like… a really big fish."

Elise: "I suppose. It's not really like anything."

Will: "Wait for it to go away."

Elise: "I'm trying."

He holds her hand.

That night Will spends some time imagining the fish. He paints it in watercolours, shiny and wet. Its iridescent scales extend in scribbled haywire shapes to the edges of page, its razorlike fins and its huge, complex, impassive eye.

He looks into the eye of the fish and feels the vortex swelling behind it. He can't see around it or define the colour of its eyes – its pupil a puncture through which outer space appears to seep.

This motherfucker. It thinks it knows her.

His love for Elise presses in on him much as water presses in on the chest of a diver as they descend.

Rabbit

Song: *Alice In Covland* by Leanne Bridgewater & Moniszko

Rabbit sat in her cage watching the children pass. She couldn't see them very well. She was almost blind. A vase of bluebells on the desk above her was blue and green, and children's shapes seemed to move through thick frosted glass.

Elise stood looking at Rabbit as the other children went outside. She reached through the bars and tried to touch her velvety ears. Rabbit's nose waffled as she searched for food.

Elise felt sorry for Rabbit. She didn't get to choose what happened to her, good or bad. She was picked up and touched and put down again.

The classroom was empty, light shone through the windows in thick streams, and Elise and Rabbit faced each other.

Elise sat at the nearest table, her shadow long and wavy. Glancing at Rabbit, she wrote down her secret, the one she thought she'd never tell, in black felt tip, cramped and deliberate, on a blank piece of paper.

Now it was outside of her in plain writing. She looked every way to see that no one had seen, then folded it tightly, pushed the paper through the bars, and watched Rabbit eat it.

Elise

Song: *Feeling Good*, cover by Nina Simone

"If nobody loves me, what's the point in living?" Rachel said to me.

We were on our break at the circus camp. We were there to teach teenagers to live acrobatically. It was a summer job, laid down in the gap before who–knows–what. We stayed in a sparse accommodation block on the fringes of a theme park, with showers that went tepid quickly in the morning. Wiry spiders moved, ghostly, agile, across the ceiling of the shower block.

I was just happy to be there.

I taught tightrope–walking, Rachel taught fire–spinning. We liked pushing our bodies, finding release in movement. Rachel even enjoyed fire–breathing, which involved holding paraffin in her mouth then spitting it out into the flame in a fine, pressured haze. It tasted terrible. She couldn't teach that skill to the teenage students — their parents wouldn't approve — but she did teach me.

When I was on the tightrope my mind felt quiet and still. I focussed on putting one foot in front of the other, the hard wire pressing into my feet, its degree of rotation and the posture I had to adjust in order to correct for this. I explained to the students how to lower their centre of gravity so they were closer to the wire and its tensile strength. Leaning forward was a common error. It is difficult to find perfect balance, difficult to maintain it; it is difficult to be patient. Success might also depend on the weather conditions.

That afternoon the students were spread out on the grass around us, enjoying their break, some still juggling and cartwheeling. A group of girls shrieked with laughter, collapsing into each other like skittles, bowled over by life.

We were only a few years older than them, and maybe their laughter only sounded bright and carefree in contrast with the shade of a cloud creeping over our patch of grass. I wouldn't be thirteen again for anything, but Rachel's ferocious heartbreaks seemed to preserve adolescence in amber. I'd never met anyone who loved like she did, all–or–nothing.

She didn't lower her voice when she talked about dying. Two girls, sitting not very far away, pretended that they weren't listening to our conversation. One of them tugged awkwardly on her shoelace.

Rachel pulled her hair back from her face and lay flat on the grass, frowning at the sky. Her profile had the austere beauty of a bird of prey.

"I always fall for these straight girls," she said. "They never love me back. It's hopeless. I need to be loved, Elise."

"You can't hold people hostage," I said. "You have to love yourself."

"How do I love myself if nobody loves me?"

"I love you," I said. "Platonically, if that's ok."

She rolled her eyes. "You love everyone. Everyone loves you. You have Will. I'm alone." She looked directly at me. "Last night I took a bottle of red wine into the shower, then I smashed the bottle and cut my thighs with the broken bits. I couldn't tell the wine from the blood. You want to see?" She laughed.

I glanced at her legs. She was wearing black leggings and would have to strip to show me the cuts. The suggestion was mildly flirtatious.

"No," I said. "But look. I do understand."

I pointed to a scar, shaped like a fishhook, on the inside of my arm. The scar was still vivid enough to make people visibly flinch, although, as it was turned inwards, they usually didn't notice it. I used to hide it with sleeves. I was getting more used to not hiding things. I watched Rachel take it in.

She didn't flinch. "Anyway," I said. "You're wrong. I don't love everyone."

"Ah," Rachel said, squinting up at me. The sun had come out from behind the cloud and was shining into her eyes, turning them the colour of whiskey. We sat in silence. I didn't know what to tell Rachel about living, because the truth was that I could have died. The rift got inside me.

The thing to get your head and body around is the shape and shame of your own helplessness. Our existence is much more dependent than we let ourselves think. For example, is the kind of depression that I experience, the kind that invades your body and steals your peace of mind, made up of a lack of serotonin, the tidal force of genetics, or the things that happen to me?

Rachel's ability to place her depressions in love's arms, as though the right woman could restore her instantly, and whole, seemed to me a hopeful confusion of means and ends. Though there was hope inside it.

*

Maybe it went like this. I was lying at the bottom of the sea. Far above, the waves broke like clouds.

Will was fighting the fish. It was formidable, with huge spiny teeth. It was one of those deep–sea fish, far beyond the sun's reach, that glows in the dark. I could see why Will had fixated on it. He thought I was trapped inside and could be saved.

In fact, I was part of the sea that held me flat, much further down. Little glittery bloody scales fluttered down and landed on me.

Will looked angry, which was unusual for him.

I watched with detached interest. Thoughts were difficult then, and so were feelings.

In a way, it was funny. He was trying so hard.

If I could, I would have told him that what held me was not an identifiable enemy but an element, like gravity, surrounding us both.

The thoughts that filtered through the sediment:

Here we are. It is dark. It is cold. My body is heavy. What is to be done.

I have tried to die.

I feel inhuman.

Fishscales flutter down on me like snow.

Will is starting to get tired of fighting.

I wonder what would happen if he drifted here and lay down beside me.

I can't imagine being a thing that he loves.

We know very little about the furthest reaches of the sea, or of our own minds.

The fish looks enraged, exhausted.

I should do something to help it. It's the real victim here.

I open my mouth. A long stream of bubbles comes out and they drift past Will in the bloodstained clouds. He looks down and finally sees me.

*

I try to sense the waves before they hit. I take medicine, follow careful habits. I hope for good conditions. I tell Rachel that as I lay in hospital, held in place in the depths, a vast weight moved over me in a heave of breath, and I was free. What can I give you other than this breath that moves beyond my understanding? I'm holding it now. As I focussed on the surface, almost beyond sight, as I rose into my life, great valves of sea opened and closed.

This World Sorrow

Song: *Sorrow* by Life Without Buildings

"I don't believe in this world sorrow."
– *A Room with a View* (1908), by E. M. Forster

Well, you said you liked cornflowers, Mr Emerson was saying. So we brought you cornflowers, said George.

They were tying garlands around the bedframes of the Miss Allens, putting the flowers into the women's hair. I whispered the lines along with them. Dusk filtered thinly through the orange curtains as I sat with my laptop balanced on my knees, watching purple–blue undulate over the screen.

Mike knocked at the door. "Tea?"

"Okay."

He came in, looked and shook his head. "*A Room with a View* again?"

"Don't judge me."

"How many times this week?"

"Five. So far."

"Come back to reality. It's where everybody lives."

I wiped a hand over my eyes. "Don't be a Cecil."

"Which one's Cecil again?"

"The stupid one."

"The one who *wouldn't play tennis with Freddy*?"

"Yes."

"That's mean. I'm much more like – what's his name. Emerson."

"George Emerson. The hero."

"Yes."

"Ha," I said.

"I have a romantic side."

"*Where*?"

He looked hurt.

"Sorry," I said. "What are you up to today?"

"Finishing my dissertation. How's yours?"

"Shhhh. Don't ask. You can go away now."

When the film was over, I cried. I am not Lucy Honeychurch, I am Megan Stubbs. I'd never meet anyone who'd run through a storm or kiss me in a wildflower field. If I ever swam naked in a lake it would be muddy and cold. I was failing at life, both emotionally and by all practical measures. None of it mattered. Into the ground we went.

My room was musty and faced the back end of a pub. I heard a rattling outside and looked out to see a fox with its thin paws up against a toppled bin. It was hungry. I wondered if it was the same vixen I heard screaming through the night. I hadn't washed for a few days. The vixen's eyes flashed at me. "Don't judge me," I whispered.

Mike knocked again. I pulled the door open. "What?"

"You okay?"

"I'm fine."

"Have you eaten?"

"I need to lose weight."

"Do you? You look like a haunted rocking horse."

"Fuck you," I said, then cried again.

"...Jesus. Come with me. No arguing."

"I'm not your slave," I said, following him miserably into the kitchen. He broke eggs into a pan.

"I can't eat an egg," I said. "Not one."

He moved the eggs roughly around the pan, scrambling them, then set it down in front of me. "What's wrong?"

"Everything's pointless."

"You've got friends. Roof over your head."

"That just makes me feel worse. The world's ending. What friends."

He scooped a forkful of egg and held it towards me. "You think I do this for my enemies?"

"Just the kind of sick thing you'd do," I said, but took the fork into my mouth.

After I'd eaten, I helped him wash up. He looked serious.

"Sorry for being such a bitch," I said.

"You're not. Why do you keep watching that film over and over?"

"It's perfect. Better than life."

"The book's a bit rougher," he said. "More political."

"I didn't know that you'd read the book."

"Yeah, well. I'm interested in what you like."

"Why?"

He didn't reply.

I looked at the tender nape of his neck and shuffled my bare feet on the lino floor, growing aware of my baggy pyjamas and the fact that I wasn't wearing a bra.

"I'll be right back," I said.

I brushed my teeth in front of the bathroom mirror. In the sickly yellow light my face looked gaunt. I had dark hollows under my eyes. I showered and shaved my legs with a blunt razor, then went to my room and pulled on turquoise underwear, a soft black t–shirt and a red skirt.

When I returned to the kitchen, Mike was sitting at the table with his headphones in, listening to heavy metal and typing steadily.

I sat opposite him. "Coffee?"

"Huh?"

"DO YOU WANT COFFEE."

"Oh – okay."

The coffee brewed. I watched it swirl chaotically. Blood percolated through my skin. Mike frowned with concentration. I looked at all the buttons on his shirt.

"DO YOU WANT TO HAVE SEX?" I asked.

He swallowed with difficulty and took his headphones off.

"Do you want to have sex," I repeated. "With me."

He laughed hesitantly. "You're joking."

"I'm not."

"You don't like me like that."

"How do you know?"

"You never have."

"Do you like *me* like that?"

"That's — not a fair question."

I walked around the table and kissed him. He flushed. The air rose darkly around us, then he said "Stop."

"Why?"

"You're not being serious."

"If you say so."

He looked wounded. "Megs, you're just bored and depressed. Stop playing."

"Oh. Okay."

"I'm worried about you."

"I don't want you to worry about me. I want you to fuck me."

We stared each other down. He spun in a frustrated circle and turned away from me, running one hand through his hair.

"I don't want to wreck our friendship," he said.

"Right," I said. Right. Right.

I retreated to my room and faced the mirror. I looked like an Egon Schiele painting. "Ugh," I said to me.

I put on *A Room with a View* again and skipped to the scene in which Lucy tells Cecil that she can't marry him, because she doesn't love him. Cecil is tall and imperious and sad, like a tragicomic heron, or a funereal top–hat. He perches on the stairs, crushed, lacing up his shoes.

I curled into a ball.

The next morning my head hurt, but I got up. My dress was clean and blue. I poured cereal. It looked like soft cardboard. Ate it. Good. I didn't know where Mike was; the flat was empty.

I walked to the park. I had to do something. My legs felt heavy but sparrows perched in the magnolia trees, and scrubby clouds drifted in the sky, punctured by whirring wings. Blossom covered the earth in pink confetti. I lay on my back, feeling insects track over my skin, each petal landing.

The clouds swirled, forecasting nothing. I put my headphones in and listened to *Sorrow* by Life Without Buildings.

There is a line *A Room With A View* about the only perfect view being the sky over our heads. I didn't know if that was true, but it always struck me as a cute thing to say. It seemed true that day. The trees rustled and waved their branches. My mind was almost still. I moved my fingers in piano patterns over my torso, spreading my hair out in the grass.

I don't believe in this world sorrow, do you?

No, Mr Emerson. Not this world sorrow. No why. No more dying.

When I got back to the flat, Mike was standing at the kitchen table with a cut–glass vase in front of him, bouncing rainbows off the walls. Sun touched his eyes and hair. As he turned to face me, I saw water brimming in the vase, green stems covered in bubbles of air, and a blue fire fanning out, every bloom etched in light. The vase was full of cornflowers.

Elise's Hospital Songs

1) Ca' the Yowes to the Knowes, cover by Joanna Newsom
2) Aquarius / Let the Sunshine In by The 5th Dimension
3) Personal Jesus, cover by Johnny Cash
4) All Along the Watchtower, cover by Jimi Hendrix
5) Moments of Pleasure by Kate Bush
6) The Real Thing by Russell Morris
7) Silence by PJ Harvey
8) The Barrel by Aldous Harding
9) Sweet Jane, cover by Cowboy Junkies
10) Sweet Dreams (Are Made of This) by Eurythmics
11) I Put A Spell On You by Screamin' Jay Hawkins
12) Falling by Haim
13) Avant Gardener by Courtney Barnett
14) Roller Girl by Anna Karina
15) Oh Bondage! Up Yours! by X–Ray Spex
16) Perfect Day Elise by PJ Harvey
17) Heavy Water/I'd Rather Be Sleeping by Grouper
18) Alice In Covland by Leanne Bridgewater & Moniszko
19) Feeling Good, cover by Nina Simone
20) Sorrow by Life Without Buildings

Acknowledgments

Thank you so much to Aaron Kent, and to the whole team at Broken Sleep Books.

An earlier version of 'This World Sorrow' was published in *ALOE* magazine (2020), thanks to editor Samuel Best.

To those who read, commented on, or quietly encouraged any of these stories in progress (Alex, Aparna, Ben S., Charlotte F., Charlotte H., Ed B., Erika, Franziska, Giles, Lena, Lizzie, Lucia, Naomi, Noemi, Olivia, Serena, Vicky, and Zoë), thank you, you helped immeasurably. Thank you especially to Livia Franchini for her vital insight on several stories, and for suggesting that this mixtape belongs to Elise.

Love and strength to those who spoke with me about their experiences of bipolar depression. This collection is fiction but owes much understanding to them.

Love and thanks to my family, especially my parents Ian Winter and Wendy Varley, whose encouragement allowed me to try. Endless love to Ollie Evans for everything.

In memory of Geetha and Leanne.

LAY OUT YOUR UNREST